LOST WITCH

TORRENT WITCHES COZY MYSTERIES BOOK NINE

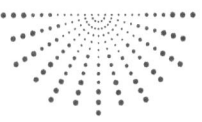

TESS LAKE

ALSO BY TESS LAKE

Torrent Witches Cozy Mysteries

Butter Witch (Torrent Witches Cozy Mysteries #1)

Treasure Witch (Torrent Witches Cozy Mysteries #2)

Hidden Witch (Torrent Witches Cozy Mysteries #3)

Fabulous Witch (Torrent Witches Cozy Mysteries #4)

Holiday Witch (Torrent Witches Cozy Mysteries #5)

Shadow Witch (Torrent Witches Cozy Mysteries #6)

Love Witch (Torrent Witches Cozy Mysteries #7)

Cozy Witch (Torrent Witches Cozy Mysteries #8)

Lost Witch (Torrent Witches Cozy Mysteries #9)

Wicked Witch (Torrent Witches Cozy Mysteries #10)

Box Sets

Torrent Witches Box Set #1 (Butter Witch, Treasure Witch, Hidden Witch)

Torrent Witches Box Set #2 (Fabulous Witch, Holiday Witch, Shadow Witch)

Audiobooks

Butter Witch

Treasure Witch

Hidden Witch

Torrent Witches Box Set #1 (Butter Witch, Treasure Witch, Hidden Witch)

Fabulous Witch

Holiday Witch

Shadow Witch

Torrent Witches Box Set #2 (Fabulous Witch, Holiday Witch, Shadow Witch)

Lost Witch Copyright © 2017 Tess Lake. ALL RIGHTS RESERVED. This book contains material protected under International and Federal Copyright Laws and Treaties. Any unauthorized reprint or use of this material is prohibited. No part of this book may be reproduced or transmitted in any form or by any means, electronic or mechanical, including photocopying, recording, or by any information storage and retrieval system without express written permission from the author.
Tess Lake

Tesslake.com

This is a work of fiction. The characters, incidents and dialogs in this book are of the author's imagination and are not to be construed as real. Any resemblance to actual events or persons, living or dead, is completely coincidental.

CHAPTER ONE

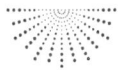

The day was crisp and cold, the sun was rising and the night security guard was dead.

"Harlow," Carter Wilkins said, nodding to me as he walked by. He'd called me at a ridiculous hour this morning telling me to get out to the mall construction site. He'd received an anonymous call advising that someone had been murdered. Believe me, although he was playing the serious, somber reporter this morning, I could tell from the twitching of his eyebrows that he was incredibly excited to have an anonymous source calling *him*.

Murder aside for a moment... yes, I was working with Carter of the giant eyebrows. After Writerpalooza finished, I was back to unemployment and writing my book. Peta had helped me out with some part-time waitressing shifts at *The Cozy Cat Cafe*, but it wasn't enough to live on. So I'd swallowed my pride, and I also guess my anger and general annoyance at Carter and taken up his offer to write for the *Harlot Bay Times*. I absolutely was *not* selling out—I'd made it very clear to him that we were partners rather than me being his employee and I wouldn't be writing tabloid garbage.

Carter had accepted my terms (plus my wage demands) and voilà—I was back writing articles and living life (part-time at least) as a journalist.

My first stories had been covering the fallout of the *Mysterious Mysteries* duo, Rufus and Dawn, being arrested, released on bail and then the case subsequently being dropped when more mysterious symbols continued to appear around Harlot Bay despite the fact Rufus and Dawn had left the state.

I cringed a little remembering those stories—I was a journalist with a commitment to publishing the truth... but I'd been forced to write fiction. Aunt Cass had been behind the new symbols, dragging Molly and Luce out at night to carve and spray paint them through the town. The idea had been to muddy the waters, and it had worked. It appeared that even some of the local teenagers had started spraying the symbols themselves, thinking it was hilarious to have an entire town on the brink of a nervous breakdown.

I'd had to work with Carter in trying to discover the culprits... while being *related* to the culprits. Thankfully it hadn't been for long—Aunt Cass had abruptly stopped the night-time excursions, the teenagers had gotten bored, and the city scrubbed, sanded and painted away the symbols. Even the *Mysterious Mysteries* had stopped pushing their brush with the law for online views and were now somewhere in the deep South tracking down so-called Vampire cults.

The national media which had been buzzing around the town (mostly mocking us) had eventually grown bored too and vanished virtually overnight. Once that happened it seemed that *everyone* simply moved on and didn't want to think about the attacks and strange symbols.

Well, anyone *non-magical* of course. We witches were still very much interested but more on that later.

I rubbed my hands together to warm them and brought myself back to the here and now. It was the tail end of summer but wickedly cold due to the strange weather of Harlot Bay and time of morning. At the crime scene, Sheriff Hardy and his officers had already taped off the area. The body was untouched—they couldn't risk ruining any evidence. The night security guard, a local named Morris Sanderson, stared up at the cold blue sky with lifeless eyes. On the front of his gray uniform was a vivid red splotch of blood.

It was early in the morning, but a small crowd of tourists and locals was already forming, along with the gathered construction workers. I took a quick look around to see if Morris' ghost was amongst them but there was no such luck. The only supernatural being on the scene was, well, *me*.

I switched on my digital recorder and began murmuring into it as I slowly walked around.

"Local, Morris Sanderson, believed age around fifty, need to check this, dead at mall construction site. Blood on shirt, no info as to how he died. Area is partially built construction site, body discovered by workers early morning."

I kept talking as I walked, stepping around a mud puddle, looking at the ruined land.

The mall construction site was precisely as Carter had described it in his furious editorials: a blight on the earth. What had once been green fields and some old housing was now a dirty wound of concrete and steel mesh stretching off into the distance. We were still digging into it, but somehow Sylvester Coldwell, sleazy real estate developer and general stain on humanity, had managed to threaten, bribe and who knows what else to get approval for his gigantic mall project. As soon as it had been shoved through against the wishes of the locals, he'd rushed to start construction, I suppose working on the idea that if it progressed far enough along it would be impossible to reverse.

Call me cynical, but he was probably right. Construction meant jobs for locals and if it were stopped there'd just be a giant mess out here that looked terrible. Carter was pursuing leads on the council members who'd voted approval but even he was beginning to recognize it was possibly a lost cause. The only thing driving him at the moment was his hatred of Coldwell, his former landlord who'd evicted him from his business premises after Carter had fallen through a step and broken his arm. Then Coldwell had done it *again*, buying the second building Carter had rented. Since then, Carter had been working out of his home. I'd been there a few times and even had a small desk crammed into a corner to work from (I mostly worked in *my* office still though—there was only so much Carter a witch could stand).

I stopped walking and turned around to take in the scene so I could describe it later. Sheriff Hardy had clearly made a decision about his crime scene—Morris was now covered up, and the Sheriff's officers were moving all locals, tourists, construction workers and reporters away from the site. Carter was waving his digital recorder in the air and calling out to Sheriff Hardy as an impassive officer gently moved him back.

I walked back to the crowd, avoiding as much mud as I could, to find Carter arguing with Sheriff Hardy.

"The public has a right to know," Carter said.

"This is private property, *and* it's a construction site Carter. It's not safe for you or anyone else to be here," Sheriff Hardy said.

Carter responded to this by lifting his camera up in the air and trying to take a photo of the scene over Sheriff Hardy's head. Oh boy, this was going to get out of control if I didn't do something.

"Sheriff, can you tell me the name of the deceased?" I called out, although I already knew it.

"It's Morris Sanderson, Harlow, and please don't publish anything until I've had a chance to talk to his family."

Sheriff Hardy was in his gruff all-business mode. He was my uncle, married to my Aunt Ro and I'd known him forever (including coming home in the back of his police car a few times), but right now both of us had roles to play. I was the journalist at work, and he was the Sheriff.

"Everyone needs to leave this site immediately," Sheriff Hardy called out and then waved to his men to make it so. Carter was about to protest, but a new development stopped him in his tracks: a shiny black car arrived and none other than Sylvester Coldwell himself leaped out.

Carter headed toward him, and so did I, but Sylvester was too fast for us. He dodged behind some construction workers and somehow made it past the police tape. He was rushing toward Morris' covered body when Sheriff Hardy grabbed him by the arm to stop him.

"This is a crime scene, you can't be here," Sheriff Hardy said, not unkindly.

"Who's under there? Is it Morris?"

I'd never seen Coldwell like this. Normally, he was a sneering supercilious horror of a man, quick with an insult if he thought no one else could hear him. Now he was frantic. His eyes were red. Had he been crying?

"It is. Please, come back over here," Sheriff Hardy said.

That journalistic fire I'd felt in my chest upon seeing Coldwell had flared and died at seeing him genuinely distressed. The question I was about to shout out wisped away.

Carter, however, was still angry.

"Morris Sanderson has died on your construction site

Coldwell. Was this due to your terrible building safety record?"

The fury on Coldwell's face replaced his distress. He lunged at Carter, his swing barely missing his nose. Carter stumbled backward and sat down in the mud.

"Assault! He attacked me!" he started yelling.

Sheriff Hardy pulled Coldwell away, back to his car and waiting driver while a few of the assembled construction workers laughed amongst themselves at Carter. Coldwell's car sped away, and then Sheriff Hardy was back, his stone cop look firmly fixed in place. Carter had pulled himself out of the mud and was waving his recorder around, ranting.

"You let him go after he attacked me!"

"Turn that off," Sheriff Hardy said.

Carter went to argue but then finally came to his senses after taking a look at Sheriff Hardy. He was about five seconds away from arresting *everyone*.

"The people have a right to know," Carter said, glaring at everyone. He turned to me. "C'mon Harlow, we'll write about this and report it to the people. Let's go."

He walked off, obviously expecting me to follow him. I felt the weight of everyone watching me, judging me silently. I was suddenly the girlfriend of the stupid idiot who has just embarrassed himself publicly and then she is expected to scurry along behind him as he walks away.

Sheriff Hardy must have seen my discomfort.

"Everyone and I mean *everyone*, off the site immediately. Construction workers to the gate. Let's go, let's go!"

As his men moved everyone away, I breathed a sigh of relief. I was still incredibly embarrassed, but at least I wouldn't be walking off with everyone staring at me. I walked out with the crowd. I found Carter standing by his car talking on his phone. He was watching me with a strange look as I approached.

"Can you tell me your name or something I should call you?" he asked. Whomever he was talking to declined to answer and hung up.

"Another anonymous tip?" I asked.

"Have you spoken with your cousins yet?" Carter replied.

My phone rang, and I felt my stomach sink. *What now?*

It was Molly and she was frantic.

"Harlow we need you over at *Traveler* right now!"

I could hear Luce shouting in the background. It was mostly swearing, but I clearly heard her say "It's a setup!"

"What's happening? Are you okay?"

My anxiety was in my throat. I started rushing for my car.

"*Traveler* is being shut down! Luce has lost her mind! We need—"

The phone cut off. A moment later I felt a ripple in the magic around me. Something bad was happening.

My car seemed to take a thousand lifetimes to start. The aforementioned anxiety was at about a million, but I was taking deep breaths and trying to hold it together. It must have partially worked because as I drove away from the construction site, I managed to notice that Carter's car was already gone.

A million bucks if you can guess where he went.

CHAPTER TWO

"Ma'am, I have a job to do, if you could step aside!"

The bureaucrat was small and dressed in shades of brown. He was holding an enormous fluorescent orange sticker in his hand and trying without luck to get around Luce so he could stick it to *Traveler's* door.

"How do you *not* see that amount of mice is sabotage?" Luce yelled.

"Please Luce, it's done whether the notice is up or not," Molly pleaded.

Carter was standing nearby, his recorder in his outstretched hand. Close enough to capture what was happening but far enough away if someone wanted to take a swipe at him. He was still wet from the mud puddle, although some of it had dried and was flaking to the ground at his feet.

"We don't even serve chicken! It was planted in the back room," Luce howled, trying to fend off the bureaucrat.

"I'm a Government official, and if you don't let me do my job I'll call the police down here so I can!"

The magic around Luce was swirling like a hurricane. If I didn't calm her down soon who knew what would happen? It's not just Slip witches who have a problem with magic lashing out. Take any standard witch and put her under enough pressure and something dangerous could occur.

Well aware that Carter was watching closely and had his recorder out, I moved closer to Luce and put my hand on her arm.

"It's okay Luce, we'll work it out," I said gently.

She looked at me, the anguish clear on her face. "But it's sabotage Harlow, and this guy is trying to shut us down!"

"As I said before, my name is Hamish Fenwick, I work for the Health Department, and this is a job. It's not personal," Hamish said.

"Just let him do his job, and we'll go inside and work out what to do," I said, still not entirely sure what had happened.

Luce reluctantly allowed me to pull her away from the front of *Traveler*. Hamish took the opportunity to stick the giant orange "Shut By Order Of The Health Department" sticker on the front door and another on the window. Hamish handed a sheaf of paperwork to Molly along with a business card.

"That's my business card. Rectify the situation and give me a call and I'll come back as soon as I possibly can," he said before scurrying away down the street.

"Hey, wait!" Carter called out following along behind him.

"We're doomed Harlow, this is going to ruin us," Molly said to me. I saw Hamish jump into his car and head off down the street. As soon as he was gone Carter turned around and came back towards us.

"Quick, let's get inside. I don't want to have to talk to Carter about this," I urged. We bustled inside *Traveler*, locked the door and then pulled the blinds down. We were waiting inside in the gloom expecting to hear Carter bang on the door, but nothing happened. I listened carefully, but all I could hear was the sound of him talking over near his car. I peeked out through the blinds and saw he'd received another phone call. I saw him look towards *Traveler* with that same strange expression on his face again, put the phone in his pocket, and then he got in his car and drove away.

That was about when a white mouse crawled over my foot.

"Oh my Goddess, why is there a mouse in here?" I said, jumping away from the front window.

"It's not one mouse, it's more like about *fifty*," Molly said. She switched the lights on, and I turned around. The inside of *Traveler* looked as it always did. There was their crazy coffee machine behind the counter, gleaming and clean, their stacks of takeaway cups, and the beautiful comfy booths where people came to sit down to enjoy the coffee. The newest addition though was the white mice spread throughout the room. They were the type you would see in a pet store. I counted at least twenty at first glance. They were all busy investigating the room, creeping around the seats or in front of the counter, climbing over everything.

"Someone must have broken in last night and sabotaged us," Luce said. I made my way towards the counter, and that's when I noticed an unpleasant smell. I stepped behind the counter and saw the floor was muddy as though someone had tipped dirt and then water and sloshed their feet through it to make a muddy behind the counter and out into the back storeroom. Sitting out in the open under the counter was a jug of milk. That was clearly something Molly and Luce would never do. I made my way out to the back room, crinkling my nose up at the smell.

"Oh, what is this?" I murmured to myself. The mud continued out to the back room where it was joined by what looked like rat or mouse droppings. Sitting on one of the back benches were a few packets of chicken breasts, unrefrigerated, a few days past their expiry dates. There were more mice out here investigating the area, but they were also joined by cockroaches that were scuttling about the place. The unpleasant smell turned out to be spoiled meat thrown in the top of the trash and left open. There were also bottles of milk sitting out on the floor.

Despite my anxiety, I put on my journalistic hat and walked over to the back door to take a closer look. There were no signs of forced entry, so maybe whoever got in had a key already? Or they could pick a lock? I carefully backed out of the room, trying not to touch anything else, knowing that we would have to get the police down here so they could fingerprint and see if they could find any footprints or any other evidence. I returned to the main part of *Traveler* to find Molly sitting in a booth looking through the paperwork, and Luce pacing about like she was going crazy, which I guess it was possible she was.

"Harlow, this has to be Coldwell, right? This is exactly what his family has been doing for generations. Sabotage some business or burn it down or whatever and then swoop in and try to buy it for an ultra low price," she said.

I made my way over to the booth and sat down beside Molly, careful not to step on any of the white mice.

"I guess it could have been Coldwell, yes, this is exactly the type of thing that he does, but..." I trailed off, looking at the sheet of paper that Molly had left on the table. There was a long list of health code violations: the food left out on the bench; the milk under it; the cockroaches; the mice; the open garbage. Whoever had done this had really done a number on *Traveler*, hitting almost every violation point they could.

"I say we go and find him right now and do something horribly magical to him until he confesses!" Luce said.

"There was a death out on Coldwell's mall construction site this morning. I'm guessing it's possibly a murder considering Morris had a large bloodstain on the front of his shirt," I said.

"Do you mean Morris Sanderson? He's dead?" Molly said in shock.

We had all gone to school with Audrey Sanderson, Morris's daughter. We'd known Morris in that vague way you know the parents of kids you went to school with. You'd seen them in the background for years on end, knew what they looked like, maybe had even spoken once or twice, but never thought about them or had anything really to do with them after that.

"Probably connected. Coldwell likely killed him himself, trying to crush the project, bankrupt it and then buy it back for pennies on the dollar or something like that. That's exactly the type of sneaky slimeball he is," Luce ranted as she paced around.

"It has to be Coldwell right? Who else would do something like this?" Molly asked no one in particular.

I sat back in the booth and took a few deep breaths, trying to calm myself. It was difficult because the magic was still swirling around Luce, reflecting her fury and sadness.

"Luce, come sit down. We need to think our way through this," I called out to my cousin.

She grumbled but eventually came stomping over to slide into the booth, picking up one of the white mice and setting it on the table in front of her. She idly started stroking its head as she picked up the sheet of health code violations.

As she stroked the mouse, I felt the magic begin to calm and finally I could put some of my thoughts together.

It was entirely possible that Coldwell had set up this sabotage and then coincidentally Morris had died out on his construction site. The sabotage completely fitted something that Coldwell would do and he'd long held a grudge against the free rent program and me and my cousins.

"Did the health inspector—what was his name, Hamish? Did he say anything about there being all these white mice in here? I mean, these are pet store mice. So isn't it obvious that it was sabotage?" I asked Molly.

"I did say something to him about that but unfortunately *some of us* got too upset, and a fight nearly broke out, and so I don't know if he really felt he was in the position to answer us," Molly said carefully.

"It's okay, I know I got angry," Luce said. The little white mouse had now rolled over onto his back, and Luce was gently stroking his stomach. He looked like he was in mouse heaven, thoroughly enjoying himself. "It's just that someone like that should recognize sabotage straight up and I don't know, *not* shut us down."

There was a thought dancing around the back of my mind just out of reach, something about the timing of all this? What had happened? I had been at the mall construction site and then...

"Carter's phone call!" I exclaimed out loud.

"Yeah, why did you send Carter *here*? That was weird," Molly said.

"I didn't send Carter here! He received an anonymous phone call while we were out at the mall construction site and then immediately after that, *you* called *me*."

"So whoever set us up called Carter so he could report on it, trying to ruin our name in town," Luce said in a dark tone.

"It's so weird... he also got an anonymous phone call to go out to the construction site. That's when he called me this morning," I said.

"So are the two things connected? Are you saying that it's *not* Coldwell possibly?" Molly asked.

"I don't know," I murmured.

I could feel that journalist's sense tingling again. Although it was possible that Coldwell had set up this attack, and then, coincidentally, someone had been killed out in his construction site, what were the chances that Carter had received two anonymous phone calls in a row, the first one directing him to the construction site and the second one telling him to go to *Traveler*? I'd have to speak with him as soon as possible. Could it be possible someone was trying to destroy *both* Coldwell and *Traveler*?

I was broken out of my swirling of thoughts by a tiny mouse snore. The mouse that Luce had been petting had fallen asleep on the table lying on its back, legs spread out, smiling in pure bliss.

"We can't keep the mice," Molly warned.

"Aww, what if we just keep this one?" Luce said.

She was an animal lover through and through, and even though this particular mouse had been part of a horde that had helped shut down *Traveler*, she still wanted to keep it.

"There is no way you can have a mouse and expect it to survive with Adams around," I said.

Molly handed me one of the pieces of paper from the Health Department. On it, Hamish the Health Inspector had written a note ordering them to block the doorway leading to *The Cozy Cat Café* next door. The note advised that as their premises were adjoined, *The Cozy Cat* would be forced to shut down unless a lockable door was immediately installed and that he would return tonight to ensure that it had been done.

"Do you think Jack could help?" Molly asked.

"I'm sure he can, I'll give him a call," I said. I left my cousins at the booth talking among themselves. As I walked over to the front door, I checked outside to ensure Carter wasn't waiting there (he wasn't) and then went outside to call Jack.

It was still extremely early morning, but the rising sun had taken the chill out of the air. The picturesque view of Harlot Bay was in direct odds to the feeling that was in the pit of my stomach and the anxious swirling of the magic I could feel from behind me. The sky was blue, seagulls were floating in the breeze, and I could hear the sound of the surf from the beach. Everything looked wonderful and cheerful except of course, it wasn't. Over on the construction site, Morris was dead. My guess, possibly shot. Behind me, someone had sabotaged my cousins' café. I took another few deep breaths and then rang Jack. Surprisingly, the call went through. Jack was still working out on Truer Island finishing up the Governor's mansion, which was now almost complete. Ninety percent of the time he didn't even have a phone signal out there, so I was very surprised when he picked up.

"Harlow, my little witch," he said, a joyful teasing tone in his voice.

"Hey, Jack, um, we have some problems," I said, trying not to crash him down to earth so quickly.

"What is it? Is everyone okay?"

Jack had been involved in witch problems before including the most recent one where we'd headed out to Truer Island in an attempt to hunt down the monster that had been hunting Torrent and Stern. He'd been with me when a man from the past, cursed to transform into a monster, had been trapped and then had broken free, flinging itself towards me.

I explained to Jack what had happened to *Traveler*, the apparent sabotage and the need for them to install a lockable door between the two premises otherwise *The Cozy Cat* would be shut down tonight. Jack told me he'd catch the next ferry back to install the door and he'd call after that. I was about to say "I love you" when the signal abruptly dropped out, and I was left standing out in the street with my phone in my hand, wondering what *else* could go wrong today. It didn't take long for me to get an answer to that question. I was walking inside when my phone rang again. Over at the booth, Molly's phone rang at the same time. Mom was calling me.

"...sit down and we can work it out! Oh Harlow, finally. You need to come up to the mansion immediately!" Mom said, on the edge of frantic. In the background, I could hear Aunt Freya shouting and swearing much the same way Luce had been this morning. Any calm I had fled when I heard her say "We've been sabotaged!"

"Is there a health inspector there? Small guy in brown, name's Hamish?" I asked.

"How did you know that?" Mom said, surprised. But she didn't give me a chance to answer.

"Quick, you need to get up here, it's serious," she said and hung up.

"I will, we will, we're coming, I promise," Molly said, before whoever it was hung up on her.

"Was that your mom? The health inspector's out at the mansion?" I asked.

"Cockroaches, bedbugs and mice," Molly said in a gloomy tone.

"Coldwell is gonna wish that he was never born. What kind of halfwit takes on seven witches?" Luce said, forgetting in her anger that Coldwell had no idea that we were witches.

We bustled out of there, Molly locking up *Traveler* behind us and went to our respective cars. Molly and Luce drove together so I was alone as I chugged along behind them, my car struggling to keep up as we left Harlot Bay and ascended the hill on the way to the Torrent Mansion. I kept focusing on my breathing, in and out, in and out. I didn't want to risk slipping, which is something that can happen if I'm highly stressed. The last time I'd slipped it had been during Writerpalooza and I'd become an ice queen, freezing anything I touched. Aunt Cass had had to make me a potion which had then turned out to be a disaster when I spilled too much of it on myself. But then she'd made me a stone infused with a potion that was much safer. That particular slip power had lasted at least a month after Writerpalooza had finished and it had *not* been a very enjoyable month having to constantly touch the stone to ensure I didn't freeze things.

In and out. In and out. Deep breaths.

Despite the fear and anxiety I could feel a small touch of calm from repeating my breathing exercises. That lasted until I was about halfway up the hill and I realized that Carter must have been talking to his anonymous source again and of course he would be up at the mansion so he could reveal the *Torrent Mansion Bed and Breakfast* was shut down by the Health Department. That realization hit me like a sledgehammer, wiping away my calm and setting my hands trembling on the steering wheel.

"Please, nothing else, oh Goddess, please," I said to myself as I followed Molly and Luce up the hill.

CHAPTER THREE

Seeing Carter parked in his car outside the mansion was bad, but far worse was seeing the Moms standing out the front arguing with Hamish. The three of them were furious but also distraught. Hamish kept trying to hand over paperwork that was being swatted away. The only saving grace to this scene was that Aunt Cass wasn't there. It was likely she was still in town at the *Chili Challenge* which was possibly a good thing, especially for Hamish from the Health Department. She had a general dislike of *The Man*, as Aunt Cass called the government and having the *Torrent Mansion Bed and Breakfast* shut down could have easily sent her over the edge. I parked beside Molly and Luce, and then the three of us went running over to where our Moms were arguing with Hamish. For a brief moment, I realized that Carter was still sitting in his car which was unusual given I would expect him to be here with his recorder outstretched capturing all this, but then that slipped out of my mind.

"I'm doing my job. It's a job, that's all," Hamish repeated. He tried to give the paperwork to Aunt Freya, who smacked it away.

"Do you really think we own that many white mice? It's sabotage!" Aunt Freya said.

Hamish turned and double blinked when he saw the three of us.

"What are you all doing here? Did you follow me?" he asked, clearly confused.

"These are our Moms, and this is their bed-and-breakfast. Someone has sabotaged them too. I told you, you should have listened to me. We were sabotaged like they were," Luce said.

"What do you mean you were sabotaged?" Aunt Freya asked.

"Someone broke into *Traveler* last night and filled it with white mice, cockroaches, mouse droppings, left raw chicken out on the bench, and a whole heap of other things too," Molly said.

"And then this guy came this morning, did a health inspection, gave us a failing score and shut down *Traveler*," Luce said.

"My name is Hamish Fenwick and I work for the Health Department. My job is to do health inspections and that's all. It's not personal," Hamish said.

I had a brief moment of feeling really sad for the guy. It really wasn't his fault at all, unless of course he'd been corrupted by someone in which case I had no sympathy for him whatsoever. But we couldn't know that. I had to step in before something crazy happened like Hamish being turned into a toad.

"Let's take the paperwork, let Hamish get on his way, and then go inside away from the prying eyes of the media," I said, trying to give the Moms and my cousins a significant look.

"It has to be Coldwell who did this," Mom said, the tone in her voice venomous.

Aunt Ro snatched the paperwork out of Hamish's hand and he bolted, heading back to his car. It was only as he drove away that I realized I should have asked him who had given the tipoff about the Torrent Mansion and *Traveler*. But it was too late. He was gone, roaring down the road. I briefly glanced at Carter. He was sitting in his car looking down, probably at his phone in his hand. I *so* did not want to deal with him right now, so I grabbed my family and managed to hustle five very upset witches back into the mansion, closing the door behind us.

"Are there any guests here at the moment?" I asked.

"There was only one couple and they left as soon as the health inspector appeared," Mom said. We made our way to the main dining room. There, sitting in the center of the table, was Adams, carefully licking a paw.

"What are you doing up on the table?" I asked him.

"Seems there's a mouse problem and seems that could be something that a cat could be hired to handle," he said, glancing sideways at me.

"You leave those mice alone," Luce said, pointing a finger at him.

"We'll get rid of the mice, don't you worry about it," I told him and then shooed him off the table. Adams grumbled to himself and then disappeared somewhere underneath it.

I became aware of the magic again. It had already been swirling thanks to Luce and Molly but now with the Moms it felt like one of those super hurricanes that comes in off the ocean and destroys everything.

"Everyone needs to sit and calm down. I don't want to slip and I'm sure we can work our way through this," I said.

To my surprise they actually listened to me, each taking a seat at the table. I sat down and took a few deep breaths but before I could speak Mom leaped up and rushed off to the kitchen. It was only then that I noticed that Aunt Freya and

Aunt Ro were still wearing their aprons from the Big Pie Bakery.

A sudden realization hit me and I felt very sick indeed.

"Did you guys leave someone at the bakery to protect it?" I asked my aunts.

"Our staff is there," Aunt Ro said.

"We're going to have to put security cameras up there. That's probably the next target," Luce said. She had that tone of voice, the one that said, *I've jumped off the deep end and I'm swimming out to sea*, but it didn't quite have the same urgency as it normally did. I glanced over at her and saw she had the white mouse from *Traveler* sitting on the table in front of her. She was stroking it under the chin as it squeaked happily to itself.

"Luce, you can't get attached. You can't keep that mouse," I said.

"If you want a mouse we've about a hundred here," Aunt Freya said.

Mom returned from the kitchen with a tray of coffees and also croissants, and an assortment of spreads. I'd rushed out in the morning at Carter's call, hastily grabbing a piece of toast before I left and so my stomach growled in hunger. Torrent witches may not be the most level-headed at times and were certainly known to snark and snipe at each other and possibly are prone to hysterics, but when it comes to eating we can't be beaten. The six of us demolished the plate of croissants, the food heading to our stomachs and managing to calm all of us. It was only a few minutes but it almost felt like it was a new day, that we'd had a night of sleep after some terrible thing, and now we could think clearly.

"Here's what we know," I began. I didn't get a chance to finish that sentence because the front door slammed open and in stormed Aunt Cass, smoking mad.

And she was also *smoking*… literally. Curls of smoke were rising up from her clothing. Her cheeks were blackened with ash and so were her hands. She waved her hands at the doors and they slammed shut behind her. She rushed into the main dining room to the head of the table and then grabbed at it with her hands. She was gritting her teeth and clenching onto the wood as though trying to hold herself onto this earth.

"Aunt Cass what happened?" Molly asked. There was a moment of silence. Over the sound of Aunt Cass breathing heavily, I heard the faint sound of the fire siren somewhere in the distance down in Harlot Bay.

"Did something happen to the *Chili Challenge*? Is everyone okay?" I said.

"I'm going to need a croissant," Aunt Cass said. Mom zipped off to the kitchen and back so fast she was practically a blur. She set a plate in front of Aunt Cass and also coffee. Aunt Cass reached down to the croissant with an ash-covered hand, took a huge bite of it and then washed it down with a mouthful of coffee that was still steaming hot.

"Tell us what happened," Luce called out, unable to take the tension anymore. For my part, I was breathing in and out, trying to stay calm. Please don't slip. Please don't slip.

"There I was at the *Chili Challenge*, dealing with suppliers, planning out my new chili garden that Will is going to help me with, when someone, who when I catch them is going to suffer greatly, threw a Molotov cocktail in through a window and into my stock," Aunt Cass said.

The collective gasps in the room I swear dropped the air pressure.

"Did you see who it was?" Mom asked.

Aunt Cass shook her head. "I was too busy dealing with the fire which very quickly got out of control. I managed to keep it contained until the fire brigade arrived but then I had to make myself scarce," Aunt Cass said.

"You couldn't put it out?" Molly asked.

Aunt Cass is a powerful witch but, like me, she is also a slip witch and that means her powers get stronger or weaker on some random setting. I've had times I've been able to hide myself with a concealment spell barely thinking of it and then others where the mere act of trying to undo a lock nearly knocked me unconscious.

"I'm not doing too well on the extinguishing fires front right now," Aunt Cass said. It seemed the croissant had helped calm her slightly because she finally sat down at the head of the table and picked up her cup of coffee, sipping from it.

"This has to be Coldwell, doesn't it?" Luce said.

"Why would it be Coldwell?" Aunt Cass said. Then she noticed the mouse sitting on the table in front of Luce. "Why do you have a mouse? Wait, can I smell something?"

I hadn't noticed it in all of the rush but there was some faint unpleasant smell. I guessed that whoever had sabotaged the Torrent Mansion must have dumped some spoiled meat somewhere.

We explained what had happened at *Traveler* this morning, the run-in with Hamish the health inspector, and then the Moms took over telling Aunt Cass how they'd returned to the mansion, only to discover rooms with white mice in them, cockroaches and bedbugs. Aunt Ro and Aunt Freya had been working at the bakery and Mom had been at the mansion, but hadn't seen anyone who could have possibly sabotaged the place. Only one room had been occupied, an elderly couple from Florida doing their long circumnavigation of the country, now finally heading south to go home. They were in their eighties and definitely in the clear for being saboteurs.

Aunt Cass asked the occasional question, her voice seeming calm, but I could see her fingers clenching the coffee cup. The magic strangely enough had calmed completely around her as though she was pushing it down through force of will.

"Plus there was a murder, this morning out on the construction site for the new mall. Morris Sanderson. Coldwell came out there and he was really upset about it," I said.

"Did you happen to see Richie Coldwell at all?" Mom asked.

"Richie? No, I haven't seen him in years," I said.

"Oh, he's been in town since last week. He came out here and asked me if I was interested in selling the mansion," Mom said. The assorted witches took a moment to digest this bit of information.

"You mean Richie Coldwell came out here and made an offer to buy the mansion and you didn't tell us?" Molly said.

"I didn't think it was important. Besides, I thought he was in town maybe for the school reunion. He left a card," Mom said. She bustled off to the kitchen.

The last time I'd seen Richie Coldwell had been in high school. His father was Sylvester Coldwell. Richie and his sister Natalia lived in Coldwell's mansion, and hey, most of us aren't *that* great at being humans at the age of eighteen, but even so Richie was in a low class of his own. All he would ever do was attempt to get girls out to his house by saying how amazing his spa was and that there was free alcohol, and that his parents were never home. We never bothered going out there, though some other people did. Richie and Natalia left town not long after we all graduated high school. That he was back in town and had made an offer to buy the mansion, which then had been sabotaged only a week later, was *highly* suspicious. Mom returned from the kitchen. As the door swung open I saw that there were a few white mice in their creeping around the place. I also saw Adams sitting up on a counter watching them from a higher viewpoint.

"You leave those mice alone," I called out.

"I'm not touching them," Adams protested as the door swung shut.

Mom returned and dropped a business card on the table. It said Richard Coldwell, Coldwell Enterprises, and then had a phone number and an email address.

"Can I take this? I'll look into it," I said. No one said anything, so I picked it up and slipped the card into my pocket.

"It must be connected, someone pulls the same sabotage on *Traveler* and the bed-and-breakfast and then they couldn't do the same thing to me so they tried to burn me out," Aunt Cass said.

"We're gonna be ruined. We put all the money back into rebuilding Big Pie," Molly said.

"I'm sure it'll be okay," Aunt Ro said worriedly.

A small glimmer of light in what felt like pitch darkness surrounding us at the moment, was the Moms had had a *very* successful summer at the new site for the Big Pie Bakery. Molly and Luce had also done fairly well as had Aunt Cass, and together they had pooled their money and poured it into rebuilding the original Big Pie Bakery. I had also been paid from Writerpalooza, and after setting a small amount aside from myself had put the rest of it into the pot as well. The bakery reconstruction was well under way and it wouldn't be long before it was ready to reopen in its prime location in the main street. As with any building project you paid in stages, but with *Traveler* and the bed-and-breakfast being shut down there was no more money possibly coming from them.

"We really need to make sure the bakery stays open and that no one sabotages it," I said.

Aunt Cass shot to her feet and slammed her hands on the table.

"We're going to make about a gallon of truth serum and then we're going to dose every single person who could possibly have a hand in this. Okay, girls, I've got a list of ingredients for you," she said.

I didn't hear what Aunt Cass said next because there was a sudden roar of magic. But this time it wasn't from me. It came from Aunt Cass, flooding outwards, hitting all of us. I was sitting down, but I was pushed back, my chair tipping and I landed on the carpet, having the breath knocked out of me. I felt like I'd been out swimming in the ocean and had been dumped by a huge wave and tumbled around, leaving my ears ringing and gasping for air. I slumped sideways out of my chair and managed to stand up, seeing the rest of my family in disarray. Aunt Cass had shot back into her own chair and then tipped it over. I think only Aunt Ro had managed to stay upright. We all got to our feet. I could taste metal in my mouth. I must've bitten my tongue.

"What was that?" I gasped. It was then I noticed that the warm sensation of magic that normally surrounded us was missing. I could only feel it faintly, as though it was at a great distance, like the gentle sound of the waves hitting the shore a mile away.

"Goddess, no," Aunt Cass swore. She waved her hand clearly expecting something magical to occur, but nothing did.

"Harlow light that candle," Aunt Cass said, pointing to a lone candle sitting in the middle of the dining table. I tried to light the candle with magic, but there was nothing there.

"What have you done to us?" Luce wailed after she tried but failed too.

It only took a few moments of experimentation for us to

discover the awful truth: Aunt Cass had slipped and none of us had any magic.

"How are we meant to find out who's sabotaging us without magic? We're not going to be able to make any truth serum are we? " Molly said her voice rising up the octaves.

"It's going to be okay. It'll wear off. It has happened before," Mom said. She was trying to soothe us all but the tone in her voice betrayed her anxiety.

"What do you mean it happened before?" I asked.

"When you were a baby. You slipped when you were about three months old and we had no magic for... what was it? A few weeks, maybe three?" Mom said, looking at her sisters.

"Three weeks without magic, are you serious?" Molly said.

"Hold your horses and octopuses and other creatures with many legs. Maybe it's centered around me," Aunt Cass said. She rushed out the front door, slamming it behind her, and we heard her footsteps disappearing, crunching down the gravel. We waited but there was no change and it wasn't long before Aunt Cass returned.

"Why is that reporter friend of yours sitting out there?" she said when she came back.

Carter! I'd completely forgotten about him.

"He got an anonymous tip to go out to the construction site this morning for the murder and then another one, I think, to go to *Traveler*. I think he got a third one to come out here."

"Well get rid of him. I don't like the media meddling in my business," Aunt Cass snapped.

"Okay, fine, I will–"

There was a faint pop of air as Molly disappeared. Mom had just lifted her coffee cup and she dropped it. It shattered on the table, pieces of ceramic going everywhere.

"What happened?" Luce yelped.

"Molly, are you invisible? Can you move something?" Aunt Cass said. There was no answer. She was just gone. Then my phone rang. It was Molly.

"Um... so I'm on top of the lighthouse. The stairs are still out and there's no way for me to get down. I don't have any magic, so I guess we're going to need a lot of ropes," Molly said, her voice brittle.

"I'll get everyone and we'll be out there as soon as we can, just stay calm," I said. I think I was telling *myself* that.

I explained to the family that Molly was now on top of the lighthouse, somehow having been transported out there. At this, a round of cursing started between the Moms and Aunt Cass.

"What does this mean?" Luce said.

"What it means is we have no magic, but I think we *all* have slip magic. So it's going to show itself at random times," Aunt Cass said.

"We might have to go out to the cave on Truer Island," Mom said.

"What, all of us?" I said.

Mom nodded. "This happened once before as well but it was only for about three days back when you were four. We made it into a camping trip and the whole family went."

I wracked my brains but I couldn't remember anything like that. I guess because I was four when it happened. My phone rang again.

"Could you guys please hurry, there are a *lot* of seagulls out here and they don't look friendly," Molly said before hanging up.

"I'll get rid of Carter. We need ropes and we're probably gonna need some other people to help get Molly down," I said. I left the Moms, Aunt Cass and Luce behind, and rushed outside to find Carter still sitting in his car. He got out as I approached.

I don't know quite what I was expecting. I was riding some edge of fear, anxiety, worry and anger. If Carter pulled that recorder out in my face I'd probably punch him. Despite the fact we'd been working together I wasn't feeling very friendly at the moment.

"Let me guess—another anonymous phone call?" I said, angrier than I probably intended.

"Are you okay, Harlow?" Carter said softly.

The gentle look on his face stopped me in my tracks and I felt a sting of tears. But no matter what, I was *not* going to cry in front of Carter.

"No I'm really not okay," I said, furiously blinking them away. "*Traveler's* been sabotaged and shut down by the Health Department and so has the bed-and-breakfast and you've been called to both locations so you can report on it and ruin both businesses."

"It's definitely a setup. We all need to talk Sheriff Hardy as soon as possible and then I think a visit to Coldwell is in order," Carter said.

"Why are you so sure it's a setup?" I asked.

Carter lifted his phone and showed it to me. "I got an anonymous tip again from that same source with a distorted voice telling me that the Torrent Mansion was being shut down for health code violations."

"Okay, but what does that mean?" I said, not quite getting it.

"Whoever it was called *before* the health inspector had barely turned the corner driving away from *Traveler*. They knew ahead of time that he was going up there. The caller must be behind it."

I swallowed and took in another deep breath, trying to find my calm.

"That's not all that happened this morning. Did you hear those fire sirens? Someone threw a Molotov cocktail through the window of the *Chili Challenge*," I said.

"This has to be Coldwell," Carter said. "I'm going to go down there to investigate. I'll catch up with you later," he said.

Then, shock of all shocks, he grabbed me in a quick hug before getting in his car and driving way down the hill. As soon as is he was gone the family emerged from the mansion carrying what seemed to be every rope in existence. Aunt Cass came to stand beside me.

"I don't like him, but you might want to warn him to be careful too," she said.

"I will," I said somewhat distantly. The list of people Coldwell had a problem with was long but I was definitely sure that Carter was somewhere near the top of it. We piled into our cars and headed for the lighthouse.

CHAPTER FOUR

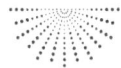

It turned out that Ollie had been in love with rock climbing when he was younger and still had all of his rock climbing gear, which was a good thing because I don't think we would have been able to get Molly down from the top of the lighthouse otherwise. All of us witches had gathered out there and Will had arrived too. We all tried rather unsuccessfully to hurl ropes up to Molly but the lighthouse is simply too tall. Thanks to the fire that occurred at the lighthouse a long time ago the internal stairs were out and so there was no way up to Molly. Even Will with his strong arm couldn't hurl a rope up high enough for Molly to grab it. Jack was still over on Truer Island waiting on the ferry and we were debating whether we would have to hire a crane to get Molly down when Ollie finally arrived at the lighthouse. He brought ropes and pinions and harnesses and in no time at all had clambered up the interior of the lighthouse nailing pinions all the way. Then he hooked Molly into a harness and together they abseiled down to the ground.

It was at that point that the girl practically kissed Ollie to death. After she'd smooched him for a while we finally managed to talk to her and she told us from her point of view she had been at the mansion between one blink and the next she was at the top of the lighthouse with seagulls circling above her. Aunt Cass had told us it was possible for witches to do such things, but it took a tremendous amount of energy and she was very surprised that Molly had teleported across town without any of us passing out, presuming it was one of us who had caused it. Somewhere in all this I messaged Peta to let her know what was happening and that a new door was being installed to block off *Traveler* from *The Cozy Cat*.

After that, we all went our separate ways.

Molly and Luce went back to *Traveler* so they could meet Jack to install the door. Aunt Cass went to the *Chili Challenge*, and the Moms returned to the bakery.

That left me driving through town with two vague plans in mind. One was to go to my office to sit and think and possibly research, and the other one was to go and see Carter at his house to see what I could discover about the anonymous phone calls and make a plan of action. I also wanted to find out what it was that Carter would report in the paper about *Traveler* and the mansion being shut down. Although it was clearly sabotage and I wished that he wouldn't report anything at all, I could see that he would still want to write about it, as awkward as that would make things between us. I guess I also want to see whether he would smear us into the ground as the anonymous caller obviously hoped. After seeing Carter act—gasp —kindly this morning I was hoping that he had turned over a new leaf and would make the sabotage the main story rather than the outcome.

I was driving along through town, pondering what I should do, heading vaguely in the direction of my office, when I saw Coldwell's office. All of the anxiety and fear from this morning coiled up inside me and turned into anger.

What if he *was* behind it? Everything fit perfectly to make him suspect number one. The fact that his son had come out to the Torrent Mansion a week earlier offering to buy it, and then it had been sabotaged was a common Coldwell practice. The next move was to make an offer to buy it at a reduced price.

I parked my car and jumped out, feeling myself growing hotter under the collar. I guess I had half a plan of being a journalist and asking Coldwell direct questions but this was too personal. This was my family and our livelihoods, and someone had tried to destroy us! I was going to go in there and scare the living hell out of him and see if he said anything to incriminate himself. I slammed in through the front door, swept past the startled receptionist and into the back rooms where Coldwell kept his office. I heard a receptionist calling out to me as I shoved the door open and walked into Coldwell's office.

"Did you sabotage *Traveler*?" I said to him. Coldwell was sitting behind his desk. Normally he was well dressed in a suit and tie but now his tie was undone and his shirt unbuttoned at the top. His eyes were still red and on the desk in front of him was a glass tumbler half full of amber liquid. There was a bottle of it standing to the side.

"I'm so sorry, Mr. Coldwell, she just ran past me," the receptionist said from the doorway.

"It's fine. We have an interview," Coldwell said and waved at her to close the door. She pulled it shut behind me.

"I don't know what you're talking about, Harlow. Why would I care about some stupid coffee shop?" Coldwell said. He was slightly slurring his words and I knew that that glass wasn't his first drink.

Despite what I'd seen this morning when he'd learned of Morris's death I was still too angry to let this go. Coldwell was a consummate liar and I suspected he was the type of person that even in the face of grief would still lie to cover himself up.

"But this is your pattern isn't it Coldwell? Offer to buy a business and if they say no, damage it and then offer to buy it at a reduced rate. Isn't that why your son Richie went out to the Torrent Mansion last week to make an offer on it? Now look at the coincidence—someone dumps mice and cockroaches and raw meat, and then calls the health inspector. Should they be expecting Richie up there soon to make another offer?" I said.

Coldwell took a gulp from his glass and then looked up at me. His eyes were red-rimmed and he looked much older than he was.

"Richie made an offer on that wreck of a mansion?" he asked.

"You're telling me your son is making offers on behalf of your business that you know nothing about? Really?" I said, crossing my arms.

"I don't care about your pitiful mansion, nor that coffee shop so can you please get out," Coldwell said, carefully enunciating each word. He finished the glass and then poured himself another, filling it almost to the top.

I had walked in with a head full of fire but now I didn't know quite what to do. Either Coldwell was the greatest liar I'd ever met or he actually didn't know that his son had come out to make an offer to buy the Torrent Mansion. The problem was it fit all too neatly and I just couldn't let it go.

"You worked with the arsonist Hendrick Gresso and his lunatic brother. You bought homes and businesses that were burnt down by those two. The police may not have been able to pin anything on you but we both know that your hands are dirty."

Coldwell picked up the glass, drained it and then stood up

and threw it at the wall behind me. I flinched as it exploded into shards.

"Morris was my friend and now he's dead. Why can't you have any respect? I'm a businessman. Of course I buy businesses that are failing or have had some misfortune. I didn't know that Gresso and his brother were burning them down. Now you need to get out before I call the police," he said. At the beginning he'd been shouting, but by the end his voice was trembling. I could feel the cold shock of adrenaline still coursing through my body and my heart was thudding. There was nothing more to gain here. I bolted out of Coldwell's office, slamming the door shut behind me, sailed past the disapproving receptionist and out the front door where I crashed into a man who was entering. I was moving so fast I actually knocked him over.

"Oh Goddess, I'm so sorry, are you okay?" I asked. The man was wearing a suit and tie, dressed like Coldwell, and as I helped him up off the ground I realized he looked quite similar too.

"You're in a big rush. Are you okay?" the man said, standing up and dusting himself off.

I let go of his hand and stood there stunned, looking at him. He had to be a Coldwell relative—the family resemblance was unmistakable.

"I'm sorry I ran into you," I eventually said. The man pulled a handkerchief out of his pocket and applied it to the side of his hand where he'd grazed on the sidewalk. I saw he was bleeding a little.

"It's okay. You're Harlow Torrent aren't you? I don't think I've seen you since you were a little girl," he said.

"I am and you are?" I said.

"August Coldwell. I'm Sylvester's brother, here to help out with the mall construction project, down from New York. Terrible news this morning isn't it?" he said. He held out his hand to shake mine and then realized he was bleeding on that side, too.

"Sorry, can't shake that, nice to meet you anyway," he said.

I swear you wouldn't think I was a journalist sometimes. Instead of having a quick wit and asking him any questions, I mostly stood there with my mouth open like a fish. August looked like Coldwell, but there was none of that smarmy sneering *I am better than you* thing going on. He seemed genuinely warm, almost as though me knocking him over had been *his* fault and not mine, and then when he'd spoken about the terrible news this morning he'd seemed genuinely sad and worried.

"You're Sylvester's brother? Were he and Morris good friends?"

Okay finally, I was getting my act together.

"Best friends since they were children. Sylvester's always looked out for Morris. It is an absolute tragedy what has occurred," August said.

"You're in town helping out?" I asked.

"Yes, well, the mall project is a big one, and now with Morris's death on top of it, it might fall apart completely. Anyway, it was very nice to meet you, and please, when you write about this, think kindly of my brother. I know you and he don't get along at all, but Morris was a good man, and my brother is extremely distraught at the moment." August patted me on the shoulder and then went inside the office, leaving me standing outside.

After some time I started walking down the street, completely forgetting I had parked in front of Coldwell's office. Meeting his brother had knocked me for a loop. He seemed genuinely kind and I was feeling ashamed of going in and yelling at Sylvester. Had I just barged in on a man who was grieving for his best friend and accused him of sabotaging my cousins' business and the bed-and-breakfast? I was lost in my own thoughts, which is why I didn't see Jack until I barged into him too. Unlike August however, he didn't fall to the ground.

"Harlow, are you okay?" Jack asked me.

I came to my senses and looked up into his eyes. They generally hovered on some point between blue and green. Today with the warm sun they were tending more towards green.

"I think I berated a man who was distraught that his best friend is dead. Then I crashed into his brother, who fell over and hurt himself."

"I hear the Torrent witches are having quite a morning," Jack said. He gave me a quick hug then wrapping his arms around me and I smelled the familiar scent of wood shavings.

"Oh, have you already been to *Traveler*?" I asked.

"The new door is installed, so *The Cozy Cat* can open. There are a lot of white mice over at that coffee shop," Jack said.

Jack let me go and smiled at me. I very much needed it after feeling like I'd been shoved in a million directions first from angry to scared and then ashamed.

"Thanks for doing that, but I have to go and see Carter now. Plus I've two–"

Jack kissed me, stopping me mid-sentence. When we parted he took me by the hands.

"Or I have a better idea. Come with me to my house and let's drink wine and smash that final wall down. I've taken the rest the day off and everything can all wait until tomorrow," he said.

"But someone tried to sabotage us," I said feebly.

"I know they did, but everyone will get the mice and bugs cleaned up, the health inspector will come back and the businesses will re-open, and starting tomorrow we can try to work out who did it. But for right now, let's change things up. Come with me to drink wine and do a little home renovation destruction."

Standing out on the street I could feel myself balanced on a knife edge, seeing the two directions the day could go. What Jack was proposing sounded lovely and relaxing. It always soothed me to work on his renovation. In the other direction was being up in my stuffy office trying to research things or talking to Carter, who no doubt would be thinking of all kinds of conspiracies. Or if not that, I'd be roped into helping clean up mice droppings.

I knew I'd be doing that anyway, but I think he was right. It could wait until tomorrow.

"Let's drink wine and smash a wall," I said. Jack gave me a kiss and led me away.

CHAPTER FIVE

"I saw Lira and I'm pretty sure I saw Tom too, you know, the one from the football team," Molly said, scrubbing hard at the dirt and grease mixture on the floor.

"Tom? What did he look like?" Luce asked.

"Oh my Goddess amazing. He was loading his two adorable little girls in their car seats, twins I think," Molly said, a dreamy look on her face.

"Ah Tom," Luce sighed.

I took my mind off the dirt and grease in front of me and remembered Tom, blue-eyed, tall and strong. He was the captain of the football team and the desire of many girls at our high school, but he was absolutely dedicated to football and so never had time for a girlfriend. Not that *that* stopped most of the girls making an attempt at climbing that mountain. After high school finished, he moved away and we never heard if he ended up doing anything in football or what happened to him.

"I wonder who he married?" Luce said.

"Gotta be someone blonde. Those daughters of his had hair so white it was like looking at the sun," Molly said.

We returned to scrubbing the floor, hard at work at cleaning up *Traveler*. It turned out that the dirt that had been smeared everywhere yesterday wasn't actually just dirt but also some mixture of grease and oil. It was incredibly hard to move.

Despite the three of us all being sweaty and dirty and up to our elbows in muck, the day wasn't so bad. It turns out a night of sleep does help and now we were already one day away from possibly the worst day of the last couple of years. Yes *Traveler* was shut down, and so was the *Torrent Mansion Bed and Breakfast*. Aunt Cass's *Chili Challenge* had suffered severe fire damage, but now we were all back hard at work cleaning up. Later in the afternoon we were going to Aunt Cass's to see what we could do there. The Moms' bakery was still open and the rebuilding of Big Pie continued apace.

It turned out that Jack had been right too that going to his house and swinging a hammer to knock down that last wall had been very satisfying indeed. I could take out all my anger on that poor wall and soon it was demolished. We'd worked for the rest of the day and then gone back to his place for showers, glasses of wine, and home-made pizza. It also turned out that Molly and Luce had done pretty much the same, Will and Ollie being clever enough to realize that taking a day off with their stressed-out girlfriends was very much necessary. Will had taken Luce to Truer Island where his family had a holiday cabin. Ollie had taken Molly down the coast to a small winery so she'd eaten a lot of cheese and drank a lot of good wine.

"What did Lira look like?" Luce asked.

"Pretty much the same. If you'd put her in some baggy teenage clothes I would have thought I'd traveled back in time," Molly said.

Despite the million and one things hanging over our heads we'd spent most the morning discussing the upcoming Harlot Bay High School Ten-Year Reunion. Being that we were at the tail end of summer, it seemed that a lot of people had chosen to delay their holidays to come back to Harlot Bay a little early to spend time with their families leading up to the reunion. I'd even seen a few familiar faces around town, people I hadn't seen in a very long time. We already had our tickets for the reunion which was being held in the high school hall and was featuring a live band and plenty of food and drinks. The three of us were excited and nervous. There was something about a reunion the made you stop and look at the quality of your life so far. What had you achieved? Had you put on too much weight? Who had married and who hadn't? Who had kids and who had changed completely?

The three of us were certainly very happy to be going with our three adorable boyfriends. It had crossed my mind in slightly snarkier moments that I was looking forward to seeing the look on the face of certain girls when I appeared at the reunion with Jack by my side.

I was pulled out of reminiscing when another white mouse ran over my hand. I managed to catch it and carried it over to one of the cages we'd set up on the bench.

I added another line to the total: twenty-eight mice captured so far. We knew there were more; we could hear them squeaking.

"It's going to be so good to get rid of *all* of the mice," Molly said.

"I wonder who is going to be at the high school reunion," Luce said , trying to change the topic, but Molly wasn't going to let it go.

"Do you hear me, Torrent? *All* of the mice," Molly repeated.

"I don't know what you're talking about."

"Oh really? Is that *not* a mouse asleep in your top pocket right now?"

"For your information his name is Hugo and I'm keeping him."

"You can't name them. We'll never get rid of them," I said.

"I didn't name him. That's just his name. Hugo Mousingworth the Third."

"He's gonna be Hugo Mousingworth the Dinner if Adams catches him," I said.

"You keep that cat of yours away from him," Luce said, cupping her hand protectively over her pocket.

Luce, ever the animal lover, had found a local pet shop that had agreed to take the mice under the proviso that they were sold as pets only and not to be fed to snakes. Despite the risk that Adams might make a lunch out of Hugo Mousingworth the Third, she'd obviously decided to keep one of them as a pet.

We kept scrubbing and cleaning, occasionally catching a mouse and adding to the total, the day drawing on. Next door we could hear the faint sounds of people going to *The Cozy Cat* for coffee and food. But even without looking, we could tell the numbers were down. That giant orange sticker on our front window wasn't making people happy at all about the food quality of *The Cozy Cat*.

We had just scraped the last of the mud/grease mixture off the floor out the back when we heard the front door open, the bell above it jingling.

"Oh, I must've left it unlocked when I went out before," Luce muttered.

"We're closed for renovations," Molly said, standing up. We all went out to the counter but stopped short at the sight of the man standing in front of us. His face was unmistakable despite it being many years since any of us had seen it. It was none other than Richie Coldwell, Sylvester Coldwell's son, the one who was always trying to use his spa to lure girls around to his house. He'd always been a scrawny kid, with stick-thin arms and Adam's apple sticking out. It seemed the years had been good to him and he'd put on a bit of weight, filling out an expensive black suit, wearing a white shirt and a dark tie. His hair was slicked back and he had that Coldwell attitude that you could see straight up: *I am better than you and you know it and I know it too.*

"Hard at work ladies?" he said with a smile.

I say *smile*, but imagine if you took a grimace and that's all you had but you had to pretend *that* was a smile. That was pretty much what was going on with his face.

"What are you doing here Richie?" Molly said coldly.

"I'm back in town helping out with some business. Looking forward to going to the reunion too. I thought I'd drop by because I have an offer to make you," he said.

"You have got to be kidding, you little fuc—" Luce said before I cut her off.

"Did you sabotage *Traveler*? Are you seriously here to make an offer on the business following the exact pattern your horrifically corrupt family has been following for decades?" I said, practically breathing fire.

Richie was lucky we didn't have any magic under our control at the moment. A spell that produced severe gastrointestinal distress would have been perfectly appropriate right now.

Richie looked around the interior of *Traveler*, sneering at it and us. As he did, I saw movement outside the door. A slim brunette wearing a well-cut suit jacket and black skirt. I groaned to myself. It was Richie's sister Natalia and she was easily as bad as he was.

"I don't want to buy this ridiculous place. Who would want it? Besides, isn't this a free rent business? You don't have anything to sell me except one thing. I came here to buy that coffee machine," Richie said, pointing at the Fuoco Oscura, otherwise known as Stefano, otherwise known as Luce's baby.

"You are out of your mind if you think we're going to sell you Stefano. Get out of here," Luce said.

The bell above the door jingled as Natalia came in. She looked the three of us up and down, and I was glad I was angry because otherwise I would have been horribly embarrassed at the state of me.

This was pretty much the opposite of that fantasy you have of when you run into someone from the deep past. You're meant to be doing something amazing, looking slim and fabulous, perhaps laughing with your adorable children when you bump into them and oh my, the years haven't been good to *them*. They look bedraggled and worn down. They might say something to you but you, *being above it all*, having moved on from the years, say something nice to them and of course hop in your million-dollar car and drive away. That was the fantasy and this was the opposite. She was the one who looked like a million bucks and the three of us looked exactly like what we were: people who'd spent the entire morning cleaning up dirt, grease and mouse droppings.

"I told you they wouldn't sell," Natalia said.

"Are you guys serious? This place is sabotaged and then you turn up a day later to make an offer on the coffee machine? Do you realize how suspicious this makes you look?" I asked.

"We were about to go to the Magic Bean to offer to buy their coffee machine too. As you may be aware, our family is building a mall and there's going to be a few coffee shops inside it. We need equipment so believe me, it's nothing personal. If it was up to me, we'd have nothing to do with your failure of a family," Natalia said.

"Oh get out," Luce snarled. I saw what was happening a moment before she did it. Luce had brought back muffins before and there was an extra one sitting in the tightly closed bag on the counter to stop any mice getting to it. She tore the bag open, grabbed the muffin, and flung it straight at Natalia's head. Natalia dodged it and the muffin thudded against the door before breaking to pieces and scattering across the floor.

"You're gonna go bankrupt anyway and then I'll buy the coffee machine at the sale. Except we won't use it; we'll destroy it for fun," Natalia said before she bolted out the door.

Richie had been grinning all through this, looking exactly like the last time we'd seen him at eighteen years old. He took a business card out of his pocket and sat it on a table.

"Call me when you want to sell the coffee machine. See you at the reunion sexy girls," he said and followed his sister out the door before Luce could find anything else to throw.

As soon as they were gone Molly rushed over to the door and bolted it shut behind them. She turned around stomped her foot on the floor, unfortunately hitting a bit of muffin and almost slipping over.

"We have to talk to Sheriff Hardy again! Them coming here to make an offer on the coffee machine is proof that they must have sabotaged us," she said.

"It's okay Hugo, the evil little snot's gone now," Luce said soothingly, stroking the little white mouse who had woken up in her pocket. Hugo squeaked at her and then saw the muffin on the ground at the front door. Luce let him go to scamper over to pick up a few crumbs. Molly looked at Hugo and then Luce, crossing her arms and then raising an eyebrow.

"Hey, he's helping clean up that muffin," Luce said.

"The muffin that *you* threw… Goddess I wish it had hit her," Molly said.

"Look, if there's anything I've learned from working at the library and all those old papers in the past of Coldwell's family is that they don't give up. It might have been sabotage today but it could be a fire in a week or some other move to shut you down. Like they'll buy the building on the other side and fill it up with garbage. We're going to have to take extra precautions to keep *Traveler*, the bed-and-breakfast, the *Chili Challenge*, and the two bakery sites safe. You might need to even think about Will and Ollie's houses too," I said.

"We have to investigate them. They want to come at us, we're gonna come at them," Molly said.

Hugo scampered back to Luce carrying a chunk of muffin. She picked him up and began stroking the back of his head as he gobbled it down.

"Are you going to help with our investigation Hugo? Can we three witches without magic take down the diabolical Coldwell clan?" Luce said to him in a baby voice.

I wiped away some sweat and grime from my forehead and let out a sigh. It was too much of a coincidence that Richie and Natalia would come here and offer to buy the coffee machine. I hadn't spoken to Carter since yesterday at the mansion although he'd sent me a few emails. I was going to have to get back in contact with him because we were going to have to use everything we had to uncover who was attacking us.

"Let's see if we can catch the rest of the mice first, and then we'll see if we can think of a plan," I said.

CHAPTER SIX

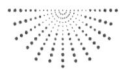

Sheriff Hardy sighed and sat back in his chair. It was the sigh of a man who had far too much on his plate and who hadn't had much sleep. He rubbed his face with his hands, making his stubble rasp.

"Did Richie offer a specific amount for the coffee machine?" he said.

"Nope. He didn't manage to get that far because once Natalia came in Luce got very upset," I said sitting back in my chair on the other side of his desk.

"And that was when she hurled the muffin at her," Sheriff Hardy said.

"Yes, but in Luce's defense it didn't *actually* hit her," I said.

"What kind of muffin was it?"

"Banana nut."

"Was it solid?"

"Oh yeah, a really dense heavy one."

I'd spent the last five minutes telling Sheriff Hardy about our run-in with Richie and Natalia, and the offer to buy the coffee machine, and how that fit into the general Coldwell behavior of trying to sabotage businesses and then buy them for a song. Sheriff Hardy had taken a few notes along the way including that Luce had thrown a muffin at Natalia.

"Well, if there's anyone who deserves a high-speed muffin to the face it's her," he said.

I laughed in surprise. Sheriff Hardy never really talked about his job, not even now that he was part of the family.

"You don't like her?" I asked.

"About five years ago I was out with one of the rookies when a car goes speeding by, driving far over the speed limit. We hit the lights and sirens and then followed it down the coast for about an hour before the driver, who was Natalia, decided to pull over. She'd been drinking and speeding, and was about the most sarcastic, unpleasant person I've ever had to deal with in all of my many years. We had to arrest her of course. We hadn't even left the scene when a fancy pants lawyer turned up. He managed to fight us on every single point, filing injunction after injunction, and so eventually the case was dropped because it was simply going to take too much money to prosecute her. So the rich got away with the crime yet again. I really wish she'd been hit by that muffin," Sheriff Hardy said.

"Molly said that too," I said. Sheriff Hardy looked back down at his notes, shuffling a few pages around.

"Look, Harlow, there is not going to be much we can do right now. Morris's murder is taking up ninety percent of our resources and the rest has been sent over to the *Chili Challenge*. I wish I could help you more. But the fact is that some mice being released in a business, along with some grease and a few open packets of chicken left on a counter, doesn't command the same amount of attention as a Molotov cocktail and murder," he said.

"I understand," I said. The Sheriff had been over it yesterday with us explaining that he was only able to send a single officer to *Traveler* who had dusted for prints and didn't find any. He wasn't able to send anyone to the *Torrent Mansion Bed and Breakfast*. The fact of it was the Harlot Bay police force was a small one and they could only be stretched so far.

"Can I ask…" Sheriff Hardy began. He stopped in midsentence and rubbed his face once more before continuing. "Is this… magical at all?" he said.

I shook my head. "I don't think so. It seems very set in the realm of normal. Just a corrupt family doing what they do," I said.

"Well that's a nice change for the Torrent family," Sheriff Hardy said.

"Is there any more information about Morris and what happened?" I asked.

Sheriff Hardy shuffled out another piece of paper and then sat up straight, composing himself into the role of the Sheriff so I could play my role of the journalist.

"Morris was shot and killed by a handgun. Forensics are still looking into it. It would have occurred around two am and it was a single shot into his heart. No weapon has been recovered and thus far we have no witnesses. There were no security cameras on the site and we are actively pursuing every lead," Sheriff Hardy said in his formal announcement voice.

I took down some notes so I could talk to Carter later, and then closed the notepad.

"Off the record, do you know what there is between Coldwell and Morris? I went to Coldwell's office yesterday and he was drunk. I think he'd been crying," I said.

"You went to his office? Oh Harlow," Sheriff Hardy sighed.

"I am still a journalist. So yes, I did, I went there to ask him some questions," I said, telling a slight white lie. I left out that I'd gone there in a fit of anger, had yelled at Coldwell and then had a glass thrown at the wall before rushing out and running into August Coldwell, knocking him to the ground.

"Sylvester said that they were friends and had been friends their entire life. I think Morris has worked for him in various positions over the years, including a long stint as his driver's since they were both in their early twenties. I think they were just good friends and he's sad about it," Sheriff Hardy said.

"Is Morris's murder going to stop the construction for a long time?" I asked. I still had Luce's crazy hypothesis playing in the back of my head that somehow it was Coldwell who had done it himself in order to shut everything down so he could buy it at a bankruptcy sale for pennies on the dollar.

"Nope, we've collected all the evidence now and the workers are already back at it. There's a lot of pressure to keep that project going," Sheriff Hardy said.

He gave me a look as he said that. We were off the record but I could recognize a clue when I was handed one. A lot of pressure to keep the project going, meant the powerful interests and possibly Council members were meddling so the project stayed on track. I filed it away as something else to investigate with Carter.

"Will you be going to see your Aunt Cass anytime soon?" Sheriff Hardy asked.

"Right after I grab some lunch we're going over there to help clean up," I said.

"If you could ask her to cooperate with the investigators that would be great, because right now she's making it very difficult," Sheriff Hardy said.

"Aunt Cass make things difficult? Why I have never heard of such a thing," I said with a smile.

Sheriff Hardy stood up and I took that as my cue to get out of there. It had been a good visit and I had gotten a lot of useful information. Although I'd taken the rest of yesterday off now I was getting back into it and I was feeling that journalistic fire in my belly that I could take to the *Harlot Bay Times* to write an article about what had been happening in the town. The fact that the construction site had only been closed for a short time and then reopened again was certainly of interest and I knew Carter would want to follow that lead.

Despite my flirting with the edges of poverty, I went to the Pie Baron and grabbed a pie and drink, which I took to the park to eat. There were still plenty of tourists, sitting about having picnics, and children laughing as they played. I was sitting on the grass finishing up my pie when a shadow was cast across me and I looked up to see Tom, he of the blue eyes and blond hair, of the football captain fame. By his sides were two adorable blonde daughters, maybe three or four years old. And they *were* twins.

"Harlow Torrent. I thought that was you, it's me Tom," he said, beaming at me.

I'd tried to clean myself up somewhat after the morning we had spent at *Traveler* before I'd gone off to Sheriff Hardy. But even so I still wasn't looking my best. Probably *bedraggled* is the right word. Nevertheless I jumped to my feet and smiled back at him, unable to help myself, which was weird because we hadn't even really been friends in high school and had barely spoken.

"Hey Tom, so amazing to see you, it's been such a long time," I said.

"You look *so* good Harlow! Are you back in town for the reunion too?" Tom asked.

"What's a union?" one of the girls asked.

"Reinyon," said the other one, attempting to correct her.

"It's a *reunion*. It's when people who used to go to school together decide to meet up years later to see how everyone's going. See who has gotten old or who has gotten more beautiful," Tom said to his daughters.

More beautiful?

What was going on here? And I look good? What?

"Who are these two adorable children?" I said.

"This is Sylvie and this is Abigail. They're going to be four next month," Tom said.

"Nice to meet you," I said to the girls who both turned shy, hugging their father's legs.

I heard the chime of the phone and Tom reached into his pocket and pulled it out, looking at the screen.

"I'd love to talk, Harlow, but we have to go right now or we're going to be late for the movie," Tom said.

"Yay, yay, movie, movie," the girls said together.

"We'll catch up at the reunion," I said.

Tom grinned that spectacular grin of his at me. "Definitely, it's a date," he said before grabbing his daughters in his arms and carrying them off across the park.

A date? Um, what? What did he mean it was a *date*? I took a look down at my clothing. I saw that I'd accidentally spilled some ketchup on my top from my pie. Okay, so I *definitely* wasn't dressed very well at all. I'm fairly sure I gave no indication that I wanted to go out with him. Was it just a turn of phrase? Oh Goddess, what had I done?

I grabbed my drink, threw my waste from lunch into one of the trashcans at the park and then walked my way over towards the *Chili Challenge*.

Okay, yes, I have a boyfriend. His name is Jack and I am absolutely madly head over heels in love with him. But still, there was something quite pleasing to discover that possibly the boy that every girl had had a crush on in high school had *possibly* also had a crush on you. Although I'd never known it and it would never come to anything. Was I going a little too far with that?

I was smiling like a fool by the time I got to the *Chili Challenge*, but that smile fled when I met Aunt Cass, who was in super grouchy mode.

"What are you grinning about?" was the first thing she said to me when I walked in.

"What are you so grouchy for?" I retorted.

"That old biddy won't help me," Aunt Cass muttered.

"Old biddy?"

"Hattie, do you know any other old biddy? I wanted her to make me some truth serum and she refused. Said it would be, and I quote, 'a good break from Torrent witches doing reckless magic.'"

"So she refused to help you, even though *you* helped *her* a couple of months ago with that amulet and that potion?" I said, slightly annoyed on my aunt's behalf.

"Yeah, well… that was me repaying back a favor so it's not like *she* exactly owed *me* for it," Aunt Cass said.

"What favor did she do you?" I asked, curious.

"Everyone is up in my business today aren't they? Can you please help me clean this up? I've had enough questions from the police and enough questions from everyone else," Aunt Cass said.

I put my hands up in the air. "Okay, okay, fine. I'm just here to clean," I said.

The Molotov cocktail had sure done a number on Aunt Cass's supplies. It had come directly through a small window, landing right in the middle of them. Almost all of the cowboy hats had been burned or smoke damaged, packets of diaper wipes had melted, the stopwatches had cracked or been smoke damaged, and the only thing that had really survived were some of the chili sauces, safe in their glass bottles. We started gathering all the burnt and blackened stock, separating it into two piles: one that was going to go to the garbage dump and the rest that Aunt Cass was planning to sell in her "literal fire sale".

"Do you have enough money to rebuy all this stock?" I asked after a little while.

"Nope. Thankfully, some of my suppliers believe in me, so they're extending me credit for a little while. But let's hope there's no slowdown, especially since I sunk all my money into that rebuild of the Big Pie Bakery," Aunt Cass said. It wasn't long before Molly and Luce turned up to help with the cleanup. I know Sheriff Hardy had asked me to tell Aunt Cass to cooperate with the police, but she was definitely in no mood and I simply wasn't going to risk it. Sure, she had no magic to use right now, but it would come back soon enough and I didn't want to get cursed.

The rest the afternoon passed quickly. We managed to separate almost all the stock into the two piles and do a fair bit of cleaning up. We were debating whether we should start mopping and washing the floors to get rid of the blackened marks first, or take the boxes to the dump, when we all felt a sudden surge of magic.

"What was that? Is the magic back?" Luce asked wide-eyed.

I tried to summon a small ball of light in my hand, but nothing happened. The magic had come and gone in a flash.

"Girls be prepared for anything," Aunt Cass said, holding her mop like a weapon.

"What is that meant to mean? Is something bad about to happen?" Molly said, looking around.

I grabbed a shovel that we'd been using to scoop up burnt boxes and held it up ready for anything.

"I say, is there any food perchance?" said a small squeaky voice in an English accent.

"Ghost voices! It's a ghost voice," Molly squealed, looking around.

"I'm not a ghost," said the small voice again.

We all watched in amazement as a small white head poked out of Luce's pocket. Her mouse Hugo looked at the assembled gathering of four stunned witches.

"Oh, please forgive me, have I interrupted something?" he said. His voice was pure English almost as though he should be wearing a small cap and a brown coat on his way to get into delightfully English adventures, and perhaps to go off to see the Queen.

"You can talk?" I said, finally breaking the silence.

The mouse scurried out of Luce's top pocket and up onto her shoulder.

"Hugo Mousingworth the Third, nice to meet you," he said.

"You can talk…" Luce said in a hushed voice.

"Oh great, a talking mouse, just what we need. I'm starting to think this entire family needs to go out to Truer Island," Aunt Cass said sourly.

"I'm not sure we need another talking animal," Molly said. Then she looked at Hugo. "I'm sorry, no offense Hugo."

"No offense taken. Might I ask if there is any cheese available?" he said.

I couldn't help but laugh at this. Providing Adams didn't make him his lunch I think that he and Hugo were going to get along just fine.

CHAPTER SEVEN

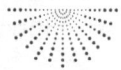

"*I* tell you... I am rocking this uniform," Kira said, doing a twirl.

It was mid-morning at *The Cozy Cat*. The place was dead empty and me, Peta and Kirá were trying to find any way we could to entertain ourselves. Kira was right too, she was rocking that uniform. We were all dressed in 1950s diner waitress outfits, pink and black with a small white apron and "Cozy Cat" embroidered on the shirt. The white socks and black shoes finished off the uniform.

"Hey, check this out," Peta said before doing a perfect triple spin, her skirt flaring up. She'd done three years of ballet when we were teenagers.

"That's amazing! How do you do that without falling over?" Kira said.

Yup, this is where we were folks. Doing spins to stave off boredom. It seemed the orange sticker on *Traveler* next door had a radius of "Eww, don't eat there" which had affected *The Cozy Cat*. Peta had even been talking about shutting down at lunchtime and going in to help Molly and Luce finish cleaning up *Traveler* so they could get rid of that sticker and reopen.

"Here I'll show you, come over here and look towards the front window and find a fixed spot," Peta said starting to give Kira instructions on how to do a spin.

I took the opportunity to check my phone. Last night after I'd gotten home and we'd introduced Adams to Hugo and given him strict instructions not to eat the mouse, to which Adams grudgingly agreed, I'd spent the next two hours writing up my notes about the interview with Sheriff Hardy and anything else I could think of before sending it off to Carter. But I hadn't received any response from him. I'd even sent him a few messages and rung him a few times but he hadn't picked up. It was like he'd dropped off the face of the earth. For a brief moment I thought he was missing, except I saw he was still updating the *Harlot Bay Times* website. He'd written an article about Morris's death out at the construction site. It was certainly more restrained than Carter had been recently, almost a complete turnaround from his hysterical reporting over the attacks in Harlot Bay all those months ago. It was pretty much a 'just the facts ma'am' article. However, it did note the Coldwell had had other incidences at previous building sites that had resulted in injuries. Perhaps today, after I finished my shift, or if Peta closed the place early, I'd travel around to see if Carter was home to find out what our plan was. I had written most of an article detailing the sabotage of *Traveler* and the *Torrent Mansion Bed and Breakfast*. To my surprise Carter hadn't yet reported on it, although the townsfolk certainly didn't need the newspaper to know what had occurred. Everyone had seen the giant orange sticker on the front of *Traveler* and word travels fast.

"H-bomb? Harlow?" Kira called out in a trill.

I slipped my phone back in my pocket.

"Yes, dearest," I said.

"Be present, you know. There's more happening in the world than on that little screen, " Kira said. She looked at Peta. "Kids these days," she said, shaking her head.

I made the very adult and considered noise that went *neener, neener, neener*.

We saw some tourists walk by the front door peering in as though they were afraid of what was inside. They didn't bother coming in.

"Yeah, well, we didn't want your business anyway," Peta said under her breath with half a smile.

"Is Blake coming in?" Kira said, now with her phone out and tapping away at it. She said it in that very unconcerned way, much like you might say "Oh, is it raining" or "How's the weather today?" The very handsome guitarist had attracted the interest of many girls around Harlot Bay. He had his own teenage fan club every time he came in to play at *The Cozy Cat*. Kira was definitely nursing a little crush on him.

"I gave him a few days off. There's no point playing to an empty room," Peta said.

"It's not empty… we're here. A private concert could be nice," Kira said with a sly smile.

"Why don't you tell Fox to grow some stubble then he could be scruffy too?" I teased, unable to stop myself.

"I did tell him to grow some stubble, but he likes shaving and having smooth skin for some reason," Kira said.

"What kind of witch are you that you can't even get your boyfriend to grow some stubble," I teased again.

"Hey, at least I'm a witch with magic," Kira said and punched me in the shoulder gently.

"So is Fox going to be working as a server at the reunion too?" Peta asked.

Various teenagers around the town had been hired to

serve food and drinks for our high school reunion. Kira, like most the teenagers in town desperate for a bit of extra money, had leaped at the opportunity.

"Not sure, he might be working at his uncle's hamburger van that night. But Sophira will be there," she said. We talked a bit about the high school reunion and then eventually the topic slid across to Tom and me meeting him in the park with his two daughters. I described what I felt had been a slightly odd encounter.

"Ooh, sounds like Tom has a crush," Kira said.

"He had daughters though. He must have a partner," I said.

"Partner passes away tragically. He's a single handsome dad left with two little daughters, raising them on his own. Then he returns to town for his high school reunion and sees the girl he had a crush on in high school but was never brave enough to say anything," Kira said in her most melodramatic voice.

"I am very happy with Jack, thank you, so if that's the story he's gonna have to find someone else," I said and poked her the side.

"I'm sure if Becky Hannigan is around, she wouldn't mind giving Tom the time of day," Peta said in an undertone. Becky had been a girl at our school, who was… let's just say *very friendly* and leave it at that. She had had an epic crush on Tom too that had gone nowhere. We didn't know whether she'd be coming to the reunion or not though.

"So Kira, word on the street is your grandma wouldn't make Aunt Cass any truth serum. What's up with that?" I said, changing the topic.

"Yeah, C-Money was *aaan-gry*. Then after my Grandma told her no, she asked me whether I could do it, but then Grandma forbade me. She threatened to ground me for the rest of my life if I helped her out by making a truth serum,"

Kira said, scandalized that anyone would dare tell a teenager what to do.

"Did she say *why* she wouldn't make her a truth serum?" I asked.

"Nope. But she definitely seemed very upset about it," Kira said.

Our witchy conversation came to an abrupt end then when the front door of *The Cozy Cat* opened, the small bell above it jingling and in walked Ru. She was Bella Bing's handler/assistant/bodyguard. She was tall, with flawless black skin and green eyes. If she was here, that meant—

"Ladies!" Bella Bing sang as she jumped out from behind Ru. She was dressed in her "I'm a movie star trying to go undercover, but making myself look more noticeable" outfit. Her giant sunglasses were studded with gems, she was wearing an exquisite oversized T-shirt that I'm sure cost more than what I made in a month, and her leggings had slits all over them, showing off quite a lot of bare skin. She was also wearing a number of diamond rings that glittered on every finger. She rushed forward and grabbed me in a fierce hug and kissed me a few times.

"Harlow, so good to see you!" Bella said. Then she turned and jumped on Peta, hugging her like she was her last and only dearest friend who'd finally returned from being lost at sea.

"And Peta!"

Ru stood nearby watching all of this with a flat expression. Finally Bella let us go and then stood back to inspect us. She looked as both up and down.

"We're in town for the big reunion. Harlow, you're working here now a waitress? I love it. You don't *care* what you're doing so long as you're doing *something*. And Peta this place is super cozy, just like you!"

"Did she call me fat?" Peta whispered to me.

"This is my business," Peta said at a louder volume. None of us had really been friends with Bella in high school. She'd been obnoxious then and the years hadn't really changed her. Then Bella looked across to Kira who was tapping away at her phone and generally ignoring her.

"And who is this? Hi, I'm Bella Bing," Bella said to Kira.

She was obviously expecting celebrity gushing but, my Goddess, had she chosen the wrong teenager for that. Kira glanced at her with that cold expression that teenagers can seem to summon at will.

"You look like you enjoy a good meal. Can I take your order?" she said in a monotone.

No one could out-snark a teenage witch.

"Did Kira just call *her* fat?" Peta whispered.

Bella's voice turned cold. "Yes, we would like some food. We can't wait for you to *serve us*," she said, emphasizing those last two words. She walked over to a table and sat down, ignoring the three of us, looking out the front window.

"I am *not* serving her," Kira said and walked off past Peta and me, heading for the back room.

That left the two of us. We did a quick rock, paper, scissors, which I lost (stupid rock). I grabbed my notepad and the menus and went over to Bella's table.

"So good to see you, Bella. Here's the menu. Would you like coffee or something?" I asked, putting on a cheerful front.

Bella scanned the food and drinks menu and let out a theatrical sigh.

"I suppose it was a little too much to expect decent coffee beans at a place like this in Harlot Bay," she complained.

I pointed to the coffee section of the menu. "Actually, Peta has gone to great lengths to stock many artisanal products including Fair Trade and organic coffee beans," I said.

I was trying to be friendly to Bella but I was in no mood to put up with her nonsense.

"I'll have a soy latte and I'll have a look at the menu," Bella said, clearly dismissing me. I was headed back to the counter when Bella called out to me. "Oh, the drinks don't come from next door, do they? It's only I saw that *Traveler's* been condemned and shut down. I mean, I'm not surprised that happened to Molly and Luce, but I don't want have a drink from there," Bella said.

Peta was behind the counter and I heard her gasp. Bella's tone was pure malice, and intended to hurt.

I turned around and made my way back to her table.

"There's no sign Bella, but we reserve the right to refuse to serve *anyone*, so if you don't start acting nicely you're not going to get any coffee or any food, okay?" I said before turning around and marching back to the counter.

As Stephano was bolted to *Traveler's* counter, Peta had been forced to bring in a standard coffee machine. She got to work making the drink while I waited until Bella called me back.

She ordered the Big Breakfast which was two eggs, sausage, bacon, beans, hash browns, with avocado, tomato and mushroom. I asked Ru if she wanted anything but she merely shook her head. Once I took the coffee back to Bella, Peta went out to the kitchen and got started cooking. She'd given Reggie the cook some time off as well now that customer numbers were so low.

I stood behind the counter and watched Bella sip her coffee as she occasionally tapped on her phone and looked out the front window. Ru was standing nearby acting as bodyguard, although there was no one around. I have to say, I was slightly surprised that Bella would return to town for our high school reunion... but then on the other hand she'd always liked the attention and where else could she get *more* attention than by turning up to a room full of your former classmates to show off your success? I guess at least with Bella being there it would take the pressure off everyone else in regards to *our* successes.

The Big Breakfast was ready soon enough, and I carried it out to Bella and deposited it on the table.

"Thank you, Harlow. Actually, I have something for you," Bella said, back to being her smiling, fake self again. She waved Ru over who retrieved a small card from her pocket and gave it to me. On it was a website address and then a code for the download of a movie titled *Witch Magic*.

"Is this the film?" I asked.

"It is and you were *amazing* in it," Bella said. "Just go there and put the code in to download it. I think your whole family will enjoy it."

I slipped the card into my uniform pocket. "Thanks Bella, that's really nice," I said, slightly surprised. I took myself back off to the counter while Peta stayed out in the kitchen, obviously hiding out and not wanting to have anything to do with Bella. It's not that Peta couldn't hold her own; it's just that if she got annoyed enough with her she'd probably throw her out, and we certainly didn't need a headline saying "Bella Bing storms out of Cozy Cat".

Bella sat there sipping her drink and not touching her food, and I was thinking she was going to finish it and leave when Molly and Luce came trooping in through the front door. They'd been cleaning next door again and looked absolutely horrific. Their clothes were dirty, their faces were red and sweaty, and they generally looked terrible. Both of them were too exhausted to notice Bella sitting there at the table as they marched in. I'm sure if they'd seen her through the window, they would have turned about-face and fled.

"Molly and Luce! Oh my, what has happened to you two?" Bella asked.

I know that sounds like a normal question, but believe me, it had a spin on it and it wasn't good. Bella had her judgmental tone dialed up to about a million.

"Oh Bella, you're here," Molly said flatly. She didn't even stop but kept walking up to the front counter, ignoring Bella.

"Can we get some food please?" Molly asked me.

Luce had come to a halt near Bella's table.

"Hi Bella, you look nice," Luce said. I saw Luce try to wipe some of the grime off her shirt onto her even grimier pants.

Bella looked at Luce like she was a timid weak animal out on the Savannah and Bella was the lion with the sharp teeth.

"Are you still with that gardener boyfriend of yours? Or is that over now?" Bella said in a tone of "Oh, I'm so sorry, dear that you can't keep a boyfriend."

That was obviously the wrong move to make. Luce held out her hand and showed Bella the diamond ring that Will had given her.

"We're engaged and now I'm going to take this ring off and punch you in the face," Luce threatened. She started scrabbling to take off the ring, but it was stuck tight on her finger.

"No, you won't do that," Ru said in a calm voice.

Peta came sweeping out from the kitchen into the main area.

"Okay, we're going to be closing up now. Thanks so much for coming Bella and we can't wait to see you at the reunion," she said.

Bella shot up from her chair, recognizing a lifeline when she saw it.

"I can't wait to see all of you. It'll be so exciting to catch up and discover what's been happening in our lives," she said in a brittle tone. Then she stormed out of there with Ru following calmly along behind her. As soon as they were gone, Peta locked the door behind them.

"Oh my Goddess, she annoys me," Luce said and stomped her foot on the floor.

Every witch in the room felt the sudden pull of magic. Kira came rushing out the back room, her eyes wide.

"What was that? That felt really strong. Cass told me that we had to watch out around you guys for this type of thing," she said in a rush.

"What's happening? Peta asked.

"Random magic spell, stay calm," I said. All of us were on alert waiting for something to happen.

After a moment there was a soft thud as a flower appeared out of nowhere and fell to the floor. It was a rose, bright red and cut as though from a florist. It hit the floor, bounced and rolled a little, before coming to a stop.

"Is that it?" Kira asked, still wary.

"Let's hope it doesn't talk," Molly said, glancing at Luce.

"It's not my fault that Hugo can talk," Luce retorted.

"I think that was it," I said, but I'd spoken too soon. Between one breath and the next hundreds of flowers appeared about head height and fell to the ground. The flood of them kept going for about ten seconds before stopping but it left us standing there knee-deep in flowers. There weren't just roses but all kinds: sunflowers and daffodils, violets and poppies. I slogged my way to the front of *The Cozy Cat* and pulled the blinds down to hide what had happened. The door was locked but if Bella decided to come storming back for a few more insults we would be caught and there would be nothing we could do about it.

"Okay, so *The Cozy Cat* is currently closed until we can get this all cleaned up," Peta said in a chirpy voice.

"I think Aunt Cass is right. We're gonna have to go out to that cave on Truer Island," Molly said in a gloomy voice.

CHAPTER EIGHT

"Kneepads? Flashlights? Helmet? Shovel?" Aunt Freya asked.

"Check, check, check and check," I said, tapping my shovel against my bike helmet. I'd taped the flashlights to it given we had no magical lights to guide us for our expedition under the mansion.

"Muh," Aunt Cass grunted still in a sour mood. Aunt Freya and I rolled our eyes at each other and ignored her. Although she was in charge of this expedition and insisted we join her, she was in a simply horrible mood and not talking to anyone.

"Check and check," squeaked an English voice from behind us. We turned around to see Hugo sitting next to Adams by Grandma's foot, watching us. Hugo was wearing a small helmet that he must've taken from a toy and holding a tiny plastic shovel.

"I'm ready to help!" chirped the little mouse.

"It's not safe under the mansion, not for a mouse and not for a cat," Aunt Freya said gently.

"But I want to help!" he repeated and waved his small plastic shovel.

Adams reached up a paw and patted it gently on Hugo's back.

"It's okay, Hugo, they don't want us around," he said in a tone that could have easily rivaled Kira's most melodramatic effort.

"Sorry Hugo, it really isn't safe," I said.

"Let's go, we know when we're not *wanted*," Adams said. He disappeared up the stairs to the kitchen with a very sad and deflated Hugo following close behind him.

"You got played," Aunt Cass muttered.

"What do you mean?" I said.

"That mouse and that cat *wanted* to be sent away. They wanted you to turn down their offer to help so they could go off and do something else."

Now that Aunt Cass mentioned it, Adams *did* give up rather quickly. He also went under the mansion plenty of times by himself and so far hadn't come to any harm… although there was one time he'd turned up with a patch of fur missing and refused to elaborate on what exactly had occurred.

"Just give me a minute. I'm going to go and talk to them," I said starting to head for the stairs.

"Nope, we have to go," Aunt Cass commanded. She opened the door to the undermansion and then stomped through it. I turned around and looked at Aunt Freya, both of us sharing the same expression. This was going to be a long morning.

"Let's get it done," Aunt Freya said and tapped her shovel on her helmet. She then turned the flashlights on and followed Aunt Cass into the darkness. I gave one final look up the stairs and decided to follow along with them. I turned on the flashlights, gripped my shovel and went after my aunt.

Aunt Cass had started expeditions under the mansion some months ago as we searched to uncover our family tree and place Marguerite Torrent somewhere in it. Witches generally don't like being on lists of any kind, having their names written down or facts recorded and so what that meant was that we were a little vague about our family tree. There was no path of birth certificates that we could easily track and even when witches did things such as enrolling their children in school, they would often cast a spell to alter details so the record couldn't be precisely connected to their children's names. These investigations hadn't yielded much and generally the only result had been minor injuries. There were remnants of old spells under the mansion and some months ago, Molly had been set on fire for a short time after stepping into one of them. Despite our lack of progress, we'd stepped up our investigations after our run-in with Johannes Tilson out in the cave on Truer Island. He'd been Marguerite Torrent's husband and cursed to turn into a monster to hunt Torrent and Stern. From what we'd gathered, Juliet Stern's husband Benjamin Mainer had had the same curse cast on him and it appeared that Juliet had locked both her husband and Johannes away to keep them safe until she could find a way to break the curse.

The curse hadn't been broken however, and so Johannes and Benjamin had remained out on the island for who knows how long. The magical seal the Juliet had placed upon them had weakened over the decades until one day, when Aunt Cass was out there alone, Benjamin had broken free and attacked her, appearing to her as a monster. He'd been destroyed, but it appeared the surge of magic had damaged the seal even further and eventually Johannes had been released. The best we could put it together, he'd been compelled to hunt Torrent and Stern, and would transform between man and monster. Johannes must've had some way to resist the compulsion of the curse. He'd attacked one man, a Stern, and then held off for as long as he could until he attacked the man's cousin, another Stern.

We'd finally trapped Johannes and briefly he'd transformed back into a man. He was the one who'd told us that dark witches had cursed him and Benjamin, due to their wives fighting the darkness too well. He'd told us to find Marguerite, that he felt her presence still. Then, as he transformed back into a monster, he'd asked me why I'd cursed our children, as he thought *I* was Marguerite.

Everything was all tangled up though. We'd found the stones with *Lost Witch Took Jack* written on them. Johannes had been Jack for short and Juliet had been the one to lock him and Benjamin away after they were cursed. Did that mean Juliet was the Lost Witch? Or was it Marguerite, our ancestor? That one of them had "taken" Jack?

What did he mean by "cursed our children"? Hattie Stern had claimed there was a spell on me but thus far we'd not been able to detect it (nor remove it). Our entire family was descended from Marguerite and Johannes. What curse could be upon us? We'd sought answers but none had come.

Most worryingly was the idea that Marguerite might still be lurking in Harlot Bay. We'd already had one encounter with a Shadow Witch who stole bodies to prolong her existence. In a vision of the past I'd seen her kill Juliet Stern's daughter Zelda by stealing her body after nearly pulling the life out of Marguerite's daughter, Rosetta. The Shadow Witch had attempted to do the same thing to Kira and me. Only the weapon left from our ancestors had saved us.

In the final moments of that vision, I'd seen Juliet's aura, normally a light gold, begin to streak black as though ink had been poured into it. I believe she'd been a Slip witch and her aura turning black like that was bad news. When Slip witches went bad, it was take over the world, hold the sun hostage levels of evilness. Other witches had to band together to hunt them down. Had *she* gone bad and Marguerite locked herself away to fight her former best friend? Was that why Johannes could sense her in Harlot Bay?

A million questions with no answers, thus far.

To add to all this craziness, Molly, Luce and I had discovered a creepy murder mansion on Truer Island that looked *awfully* similar to our mansion, hidden by a concealment spell. We'd been led out there by a map we'd found in an abandoned room under the mansion.

Out at the creepy mansion, we'd almost wandered down a set of stairs to who knows what end before I'd realized the three of us were under the influence of a spell. We'd bolted out of there and escaped. As soon as we left the concealment spell we were unable to find the mansion again but we knew it was out there—hiding behind magic.

"Watch your step," Aunt Freya said.

I'd been following close behind her, walking where she did but I'd wandered off course thanks to being lost in my thoughts. I was about to step into a hole in the floor. I peered down into it, my flashlights illuminating a dusty old dining room, complete with ornate candelabra sitting on a long table that was holding up well despite its age.

"Keep up, we have a lot of work to do," Aunt Cass grunted. She walked off without waiting for us.

Aunt Freya and I shared that same look again and followed behind. This time I kept my mind on what I was doing—I didn't want to fall down a hole and break a leg.

I'd like to say that we witches had a methodical approach to exploring the undermansion but it wasn't possible thanks to the magical nature of our mansion. Walk down a corridor and turn left on one day and you'd arrive at a bedroom. Do the same thing the next day and you'd hit a blank wall or a corridor stretching off into the distance, seemingly without end. There was even another entire floor below us and countless rooms.

Despite the confusing magical corridors, Aunt Cass managed to lead us to the ropes and harnesses she'd set up. We hooked ourselves in and lowered down to the bottom floor. Last time I'd come down here with her and mom, the single door had led to a small corridor that led to a T-junction. We stepped out of our harnesses and followed Aunt Cass. We went out into a corridor that was lined on both sides with doors.

Like... *hundreds* of them.

"Oh great," Aunt Freya muttered.

"This is gonna take forever," I complained.

Aunt Cass pointed a finger at me. "You, chatterbox, pick a door."

She was still being her sour grumpy self and I'd abruptly had enough.

"What is *with* you today! I know the *Chili Challenge* got hit but so did *Traveler* and the mansion and we're dealing with it. You have the right to be upset but not so mean for all this time!"

It had come out of nowhere and I was expecting Aunt Cass to shout at me or snark back... but instead she crumpled.

"It's Artemis," she said, trying to wipe away sudden tears.

I've really only seen Aunt Cass cry properly one time—when Grandma April unfroze for a moment before returning to her statue-like state. It seemed impossible that Aunt Cass who sold illegal fireworks and had a secret lab under the house and imported possibly illegal hot chili sauces into the country would be crying... and over a man, too!

"Uh... what happened?" Aunt Freya finally managed to say.

Aunt Cass sniffed and wiped her eyes again.

"I think it's over between us. He just… turned cold. I don't know why. Things were going well, we were laughing a lot, our sex life was—"

"I don't want to hear about that!" Aunt Freya said.

Aunt Cass glared at her.

"Good. Wonderful. Spectacular," she said, making sure to enunciate every syllable.

"Did he know you're a witch?" I asked.

Aunt Cass shook her head. "He didn't know. I was thinking about telling him because it was all going so well… but then it was like his love was switched off. Just like that." She snapped her fingers, the sound echoing in the room.

The three of us looked at the floor then as our great unspoken fear slithered into the room. Torrent Witches had a hard time keeping their men. My own father had left, along with Molly and Luce's long ago. Aunt Cass had never married, never had any children of her own (although to be fair, Aunt Cass said this was a choice she'd made after seeing the Moms arrive. She was more than happy to be an aunt to three girls rather than carry on the family line herself).

Artemis turning cold was… shocking. He was one of those adorable old men who had moments of cheekiness and was a lot of fun. He still ran his tour boat business and from everything we'd seen, he and Aunt Cass had got on like a house on fire.

Aunt Cass sighed and then clapped her hands.

"Okay, enough emotions for the day, let's get moving," she said.

I pulled myself away from sad thoughts about men leaving and gave Aunt Cass a quick hug. She accepted it for a moment before slipping away.

"Good, good, let's go," she said, opening the nearest door.

"Oh my Goddess," Aunt Freya gasped.

"Jackpot!" Aunt Cass said.

"Is that a map?" I asked.

The room was lined with bookshelves but they weren't filled with books. Shiny weapons gleamed from every shelf. There were axes, crossbows, old rifles and swords. There was a long table in the center of the room that was covered in an assortment of bottles and spell ingredient bags. On the back wall was a large hand-drawn map of Harlot Bay, Truer Island and most of North Carolina.

I stepped forward but hit Aunt Cass's arm holding me back.

"There could be dangerous spells here, wait a minute while I think," she said.

Oh, right, our severe *lack* of magic when we wanted it and severe *excess* of magic when we didn't. Yesterday after *The Cozy Cat* had filled with flowers, we'd spent the rest of the afternoon bagging them up and transporting them back home. We'd taken them behind the mansion and dumped all of them into an old dried-up well. It had taken the entire day to clear out the café and as a result I hadn't been able to get in contact with Carter again. None of us witches had done anything more than eat a quick dinner and collapse, exhausted. It turned out that moving that many flowers was extraordinarily hard work.

"Do you have a plan?" I asked.

"Throw the shovel in," Aunt Freya said and then did just that without waiting for an answer.

"No!" Aunt Cass yelled as the shovel clanged to the wooden floor.

We all held our breath… but nothing happened.

"If we feel a spell or see anything weird, we run," Aunt Cass warned and then stepped into the room.

Aunt Freya and I carefully followed. Due to Aunt Cass's slip we couldn't feel the magic as we usually did. Normally it was ever present, a flow that moved around us, like standing in a warm ocean. Now it was either entirely absent or a faint sound in the distance. No matter how careful we were, the chances we'd be able to feel any spells down here was low.

Aunt Cass headed straight for a wicked-looking black crossbow. She pulled it off the shelf, grabbed a bolt and in ten seconds flat had cocked it.

"Ooh baby," she whispered, sounding slightly maniacal. She held it to her shoulder and sighted down the room before pulling the trigger. The bolt thudded into a wooden target that had been nailed to the back wall.

"Aunt Cass, no crossbows! I don't want to get shot! We need to be safe!" Aunt Freya said.

Her credibility was slightly strained by the giant sword she was holding and waving a little too much for my liking.

"No weapons for no one!" I called out, although there was a shiny mace that I was itching to pick up.

Aunt Cass and Aunt Freya reluctantly put down their weapons.

I pulled out my phone and started taking photos of the room and map at the back. Last time I'd been in a pristine room under the mansion it had aged and turned to ruin soon after. The only thing we'd saved was the leather map that eventually had led me, Molly and Luce to the creepy mansion on Truer Island.

"This is a goldmine," Aunt Cass breathed from beside me as we all gathered around the map. The strange looping symbol that had appeared all over town was drawn in red ink on the map.

"Looks like they were tracking witches gone bad and other nasty things," Aunt Freya said. She was carefully paging through an old leather-bound journal she'd found.

"They?" I asked.

"Marguerite and Juliet. Your vision was true—they were Hunters."

"Let's shift all of this out of here before this room vanishes forever," Aunt Cass said.

It was easier said than done. I had to go back to the main house on my own and call the Moms and my cousins back home. Despite Aunt Cass's insistence that this discovery was more important than anything else, Mom and Aunt Ro wanted to stay at the bakery and my cousins wanted to finish cleaning up *Traveler*.

"We found a map, weapons and that strange symbol is everywhere. Come home now!"

Eventually everyone returned and then we set up a line of witches to move everything out of the bottom room. We couldn't risk leaving it or letting it out of our sight lest it vanish. So we had Mom in the room, Aunt Freya and Luce ferrying weapons to the buckets tied to ropes, me and Molly hauling them up and then taking them upstairs, and Aunt Cass doing a lot of telling everyone what to do without appearing to do much work herself.

Finally we had everything upstairs and piled in the room off to the side of the dining room. We'd all taken multiple photos of the map in case it crumbled or vanished. We were all tired, resting in assorted chairs.

"We're going to have to find somewhere else to store all this so we can reopen," Mom commented, looking over the assorted weapons, potion bottles and ingredients.

Aunt Cass stuck the map up on the whiteboard that we'd left sitting around since the last big family meeting. She turned to us, her eyes gleaming.

"Hypothesis: Marguerite and Juliet were Hunters. Tracking down evil witches and worse monsters. They marked their sites on this map. They fought the dark and sometimes the dark fought back!"

"Like when the Shadow Witch used Rosetta's lifeforce to

take Zelda's body!" Luce said, joining Aunt Cass in jumping off the deep end.

"Their husbands were cursed into monsters, bound to kill Stern and Torrent and Juliet had no choice but to lock them away," Molly added, slipping readily into the madness.

I leaped up from my chair, carried away in the moment. "And then... someone carved *Lost Witch Took Jack* into stones as... a warning?" I was getting too excited, so I sat myself down again.

"We don't know. Maybe it was a warning. We don't know what happened to Marguerite and Juliet in the end. We don't know why Johannes said Marguerite cursed her children or why he could feel her still in Harlot Bay. But if I were to put money on it, I bet that mansion out on Truer Island holds answers," Aunt Cass said.

"We're going to have to go out there," Mom said. "How about now?"

I found myself reaching for a short sword when the sudden slamming of a car door woke me up. What was I doing? Were we all really about to go hunting for a magically concealed house on Truer Island with zero planning?

Oh, and zero *magic*?

"We can't go out there yet, we don't have any magic," I said, my tongue feeling thick in my mouth. It was like I was trying to talk through cotton balls.

"You Torrent witches," Sheriff Hardy said from the doorway.

"Hi darling," Aunt Ro said automatically and attempted to hide a cudgel behind her back.

"As Sheriff, I'm not here and did not see all these illegal weapons. But as a family member... what is going on?"

All of us talked a mile a minute at Sheriff Hardy about finding the room, the weapons, the map and the guesses we had about our ancestor, Marguerite. Despite the flood of chatter, he simply nodded and listened. His calming influence eventually spread out to the rest of us and I know I wasn't the only one suddenly aware that we'd been recklessly planning to arm ourselves and head off on a dangerous quest.

Was it a spell pushing us? I couldn't think straight.

"Let's take all this into the cottages behind the mansion. Split them up, store them away," Aunt Cass said.

She looked troubled, I'm sure wondering if there was a spell on these weapons that we were unaware of.

This time we used the trunks of our cars to move the weapons down to the far end of the mansion. Then we loaded up two wheelbarrows and distributed them between the various abandoned cottages and buildings out behind the mansion.

"Did you really want to go on the attack just before?" Molly asked me as the three of us laid out assorted crossbows and knives on the floor of one of the cottages.

"I definitely did. It felt *right*, like I was going to battle evil or something," Luce said.

"Let's get it done and leave it until our magic returns so we can work out what to do," I said. I was trying not to think about the weight of the crossbow I was holding. It felt good in my hands.

Soon all the weapons, potion bottles and bags of ingredients were stashed away. It was late in the afternoon and we were all tired. Mom, Aunt Freya and Aunt Cass went back to their end of the mansion. Sheriff Hardy yelled out "Stay safe!" before taking Aunt Ro away with him back to their home.

That left me, Molly and Luce to troop inside our end of the mansion to discover complete chaos.

"What is that guard man shouting about?" Adams grumbled from his position in front of the fridge on the floor.

Hugo was asleep beside him, his white fur stained with food.

"Adams, what have you done!" I yelled.

"Hugo, how could you?" Luce yelled even louder.

There were food wrappers spread everywhere. Every jar and bottle in the fridge had been opened. There was milk pooling in the kitchen, half-chewed pickles on the counter and gnawed vegetables everywhere. Every cupboard door was open.

Hugo groaned awake and tried to roll over but his belly was so full it took him three tries to get upright.

"We justs whanted a schnack," he slurred and then burped.

"They've been drinking our wine!" Molly shrieked.

Luce rushed over and picked up Hugo. "How much did you have to drink? Are you okay?"

"It wassh jus a bottle o' red and bottle o' white," Huge said and burped.

"You are grounded for a million years and that's for starters," I said to Adams but I don't think he heard me—he was asleep again.

"I told you that mouse was trouble," Molly said, pointing at Hugo.

"He's probably having a difficult time adapting to his new life as a talking and intelligent mouse," Luce protested.

I made my way over to the kitchen, careful to avoid scattered green olives and a few half-eaten mandarins. I prodded Adams with my foot until he woke up.

"Can magical cats clean?" I asked him, my voice somewhere down at sub-zero.

"Cats don't clean!" Adams said, alarmed. He sat up, licked a shoulder, burped and then walked off around the kitchen counter. I dived to grab him but he was too quick. He didn't emerge—clearly deciding that making himself scarce was the right move.

"They have literally eaten or bitten everything we have. I can't deal with this now, I'm going to Ollie's," Molly said, closing the fridge door. She turned about face and was gone a moment later out the front door.

"I've spent all day cleaning at *Traveler*... I can't," Luce said.

I looked around at the mess and couldn't face it myself. I knew it would be worse tomorrow but I'd spent all day hauling weapons and I didn't have any more energy.

"I'm going to Jack's. We can clean this tomorrow," I said.

Luce took the drunken Hugo with her. I grabbed some more clothes, messaged Jack that I was on my way and left the mess behind me.

Driving down the hill to town I had to open the window so the breeze could help me stay awake. It seemed the day of hard labor was finally catching up with me. My phone chimed a message from Carter telling me to urgently call him but there was just no way that was going to happen.

I'd had enough of mess—enough of mysterious witches from the past, enough of Carter, all the Coldwells, enough of Bella Bing, enough of *literal* mess in *Traveler*, the *Torrent Mansion Bed and Breakfast* and now our home.

I was starting to think Jack had the right idea when he told me it could all wait. Sadly there were no more walls to smash down at his house he was renovating so I'd have to settle for food and wine instead... which sounded really lovely, actually.

Jack met me at the door and took me inside like I was a natural disaster survivor. Soon I had a glass of white wine in my hand, beef stew and mashed potato on a plate in front of me, and Jack rubbing my shoulders with his strong hands while I groaned and tried to talk about my day.

"So the Torrent Mansion held an armory? I wish I could

say I was surprised," Jack said, leaning down to give me a kiss on the cheek.

"Aunt Cass is surprisingly good with a crossbow," I murmured, my eyes closed. Jack gave me the quick karate chops on the shoulders and then sat down so we could eat.

"So how was your day?" I finally asked, once I'd wolfed down most of my delicious meal.

"Good... I installed two security cameras at *Traveler*, another one at *The Cozy Cat* and I put two up watching the new Big Pie Bakery site. It's not going to stop anything but at least we'll have a chance of catching anyone who tries."

I smiled at Jack, the wine and stew and my love all combining into pure bliss. He was a good man.

All the good men leave a tiny voice whispered.

It unsettled me and I took a hasty sip of wine that went the wrong way. Once I finished coughing wine out of my nose that bliss was almost gone.

"It's going to be okay Harlow. I'm with you," Jack said, seeming to read my mind.

"I know," I said... although I didn't know.

My phone rang, Molly calling.

"We need you to go to Ollie's to get his climbing ropes and stuff. We'd need a pulley or something like that too. We're up on the top of the lighthouse and so is our bed," Molly said in a rush.

I could hear seagulls cawing over the phone.

I pinched the bridge of my nose and sighed. "Magic moved you *and* Ollie to the top of the lighthouse?"

"Yes! Now hurry and I need you to bring clothes for both of us too. Get Jack and Will and Luce because the bed is going to be hard to get down."

I must have been tired because I wasn't quite getting it.

"Did the magic move you but not your clothes?" I asked, confused.

"We. Are. On. Top. Of. The. Lighthouse. With. Our. Bed. Under. Our. Sheets. With. No. Clothes. Hurry up and get out here!" Molly said before hanging up.

Oh.

"What happened?" Jack asked.

He was topping up his glass of wine. I reached out to stop him.

"We're gonna need that when we get back," I said.

CHAPTER NINE

I yawned and tried to focus on my novel, but my office was warm and I hadn't had enough sleep from being up late last night helping rescue Molly and Ollie from atop the lighthouse.

The first part of the rescue had gone reasonably well. Jack and I had driven around to Ollie's where Jack had picked the lock of the door so we could go in and gather Ollie's rock climbing equipment. We'd rallied Will and Luce and then met them out at the lighthouse. It had taken us a few tries but eventually we managed to get a rope up to Ollie and so the first thing we sent up was the clothing that we'd brought with us. Once they were dressed Ollie hauled the rest of the rock climbing equipment up the rope and soon he and Molly were back on the ground. Then it was time to get the bed down.

We had flashlights but it was still pitch dark out at the lighthouse. Despite this, Ollie scrambled back up to the top, tied up his mattress with a whole lot of rope, and used the pulley that we'd brought with us, and then with all of us holding the other end of the rope, we managed to lower it to the ground and load it into the back of Jack's truck. He'd done the same with his bed frame but when it was halfway down, we heard a snapping sound from high above us as something in the lighthouse gave way. We had to all leap out of the way as Ollie's bed frame crashed to the ground and broke into about a million pieces. Once Ollie was back on the ground the six of us then spent the next half hour gathering up wrecked shards of his bed and dropping them in the back of Will's truck who said he'd take it away to dispose of it.

It was fair to say that throughout this Molly was so tensed up she was vibrating. Sure, she was engaged to Ollie, but the worry that he might leave if exposed to too much witchiness had never gone away. And being transported naked out to the top of the Truer Island lighthouse? That was *way* too much witchiness.

Jack and I had taken Ollie and Molly back to his home, helped them move the mattress inside and then said goodbye. I'd given my cousin a hug but it was like hugging a rock. She was solid and tense, fearful and a little bit angry too. We'd said goodbye and then come home where both of us had crashed into bed. I'd had a night of restless sleep full of strange dreams of being out at the dark lighthouse, mixed together with finding the mess up at our the end of the mansion. Then Jack had left early in the morning to go out to Truer Island for work as it was promising to be a warm day and I couldn't get back to sleep. So now here I was in my office trying to do something useful but yawning every two minutes.

I jumped up from my seat and walked over to the window to open it. It was only slightly cooler outside, but it was still that beautiful warm tail end of Summer and so there wasn't enough of a temperature difference to wake me up. There was a slight breeze though, and I stood at the window, taking deep breaths, trying to wake myself before returning to my computer.

I had written about three-quarters of my novel and was slowly making my way to the end. I'd been reading parts of it and pondering titles. *Ghost Girl*. *Girl Gone Ghost*. *The Ghost Of Us*. None of them seemed right. After sitting there for another ten minutes trying to read but mostly staring blankly, I closed it down and swam out onto the Internet. There was still a lot of research to be done. There was Sylvester Coldwell; August Coldwell; what Richie and Natalia Coldwell had been up to; background on Morris Sanderson. I'm sure that the Coldwells were somehow tangled up in everything that had happened to the Torrent Mansion, *Traveler* and the *Chili Challenge*. I was getting ready to start my research when I heard footsteps and then there was a rap on the door.

"Come in!" I called out, thankful for any interruption.

It was Jonas and he wasn't looking happy.

"Do you have a moment to talk?" he asked.

"Come in, of course I do," I said. Jonas came in and sat down on the old sofa, raising a small cloud of dust. My poor office had been abandoned for quite a while and then I hadn't cleaned it. He didn't seem too worried though.

"Have you been investigating August Coldwell?" Jonas asked.

I gave a double blink, for an absurd moment my tired brain thinking that Jonas had been spying on me and knew what I was doing. Then of course I came to my senses. Jonas was a real estate developer as well, but a good one. He'd been strongly opposed to the mall and had argued against it, both in Carter's newspaper and at council meetings. He despised Coldwell for being the type of corrupt sleazy developer who had given his entire profession a bad name.

"I haven't looked into him much. I briefly met him not

too long ago at Sylvester's office. Carter's been doing more research than me," I said.

That reminded me that I needed to call Carter. We'd been out of touch for days now.

"Doesn't it seem strange to you that Morris is murdered on the building site and then the next day construction continues like nothing happened?" Jonas asked.

I shrugged. "I guess it is. It's a major project that is employing a lot of people. Maybe the police got all the evidence they needed so there's no reason to hold it up. The project still has full approval thus far," I said, playing a little bit of the devil's advocate.

Jonas tilted his head to the side and looked at me. His eyes were the same as Jack's hovering on that point between blue and green and sometimes when he moved he reminded me of Jack. "I don't think you really believe that. You know he's corrupt and something highly suspicious is going on out there. Since I learned that August Coldwell is back in town I asked around a bit and he's definitely as bad as his brother. I think he's bad in that extra way too in that he *never* gets caught, and so it's only hints and rumors. I'm not sure why he's back in town but I'm going to bet you that *Traveler*, *The Cozy Cat* and the mansion being shut down and the *Chili Challenge* being firebombed are all connected. If they think they can get away with having *The Cozy Cat* shut down they have another thing coming," Jonas said.

I nodded, not quite sure what to say. Of course, I could see his point. The Coldwells were corrupt. Their entire family had been for decades. But Jonas seemed especially upset about it. Sure, *The Cozy Cat* was shut down but voluntarily and Peta was taking it in her stride, helping out clean up *Traveler* so both places could reopen. I guess Jonas was extra angry that his girlfriend's café couldn't be open for business.

"Did you have anything specific that we can look into? If we're going to nail Sylvester or August Coldwell, we need specific things and proof as well," I said gently.

"I might have something in a few days. I have a friend who lives in a town where August Coldwell was working for a few years. As soon as I told the story of the sabotage and the offer to buy they knew exactly what I was talking about. They're looking into it now, seeing if anyone affected will come forward. If we can get something solid then you and Carter can publish it and we can take those two evil men down once and for all."

I couldn't sense magic at the moment but I could swear I could almost feel a chill coming off Jonas.

"Well as soon as you find something let me know. Carter and I are investigating and we'll do our best," I said. Jonas stood up and brushed the dust off his pants. At the door he turned around. "Sylvester Coldwell is evil. You need to be careful. Frankly, if he took a long walk off a short pier we'd all be better off," he said. He closed the door behind him and then I listened to his heavy tread go down the stairs and then heard the sound of him going into his office.

I went back to my computer with a renewed sense of purpose. Jonas's visit was like a shot of caffeine and a bucket of ice water at the same time. It had been easy with everything else that had been going on to forget just how serious the attack on the *Chili Challenge* had been. An actual Molotov had been thrown through the window while Aunt Cass was there. That could have easily resulted in death. Although the sabotage on *Traveler* and the Torrent Mansion hadn't been as bad as that, who knew what might come next?

I guess that seeing how distressed Sylvester had been at the death of Morris, I'd made some assumption that perhaps he hadn't been behind the sabotage. But then I realized it was because I was *assuming* he had a good side to him. That somehow seeing him upset meant that he couldn't have done something evil. But that just wasn't true at all.

With that in mind, I headed out to the Internet. First of all I found the card that Richie Coldwell had left behind at *Traveler* and also the one that he'd given mom when he'd come out to make an offer in the mansion. They were both identical with the name Richard Coldwell and then Coldwell Enterprises written underneath it, along with a phone number and email address. I discovered that Coldwell Enterprises was August Coldwell's business and not Sylvester's, as I'd assumed. Okay, so was there something there? Richie wasn't working for his dad, but rather his uncle. I could see that. I loved mom but if it really came down to it, I'd much rather work with Aunt Ro or Aunt Freya than her directly. There was always something about a parent and how they were able to press your buttons, buttons *they themselves* had built into you when you were a child.

I spent the next hour digging into the Coldwell family. It seemed that both Richie and Natalia had gone to work for August Coldwell, essentially moving into the family businesses directly out of high school once they had left Harlot Bay. When I looked into August Coldwell I discovered that Jonas was right. There were some hints that he was perhaps corrupt, but it was only ever implied. There were a few lawsuits from residents of buildings he owned that had been settled and sealed. Mention of Coldwell Enterprises buying a building that six months earlier had had a health code violation. Given what I knew about the family, I don't think I was going too far to assume that August Coldwell followed the same method that Sylvester did and their entire family. The fact that I couldn't find much evidence implicating August just spoke to how good he was at it.

I stood up from my chair and went to the fridge to get a glass of water and then went over to the window again to ponder things. I took a deep breath of air and then started walking around my office talking aloud.

"So August is the older brother, and is much worse than Sylvester. He comes to town and learns that Sylvester has already had run-ins with the Torrents and maybe August has business plans here too. He decides to help out his brother and arranges the sabotage of *Traveler*, the bed and breakfast and the firebombing. But then…"

Yes, but what then? I didn't know what would happen next. The bed and breakfast had been cleaned up almost completely, and so was *Traveler*. Molly and Luce were planning on calling the health inspector back any day now so they could hopefully pass their inspection and reopen. They certainly had no desire to sell to August Coldwell. Was he maybe hoping that the giant orange sticker on the front window would permanently damage their sales? Perhaps he was playing the long game, hoping that in a year from now they would finally give in and he could buy their business safe in the knowledge that the crime that had crippled them was in the past. I was standing at the window, sipping my water when I heard more footsteps on the stairs and then a knock.

"Come in," I called out.

A woman shouldered the door open and then turned around. It was Constance Osterman, the librarian that I'd worked with when I had my part-time job at the library helping Ollie sort papers. She was carrying two huge boxes full of files.

"Hey, Harlow," she puffed. She walked in and put the files down on the sofa. Right behind her was Carter hauling two large boxes of his own. I'm trying not to be mean right now, but he didn't look good. He had huge bags under his eyes, which are also red. He had a few days' stubble and there was a pallor to his skin. He was yawning as it hauled the boxes in and then put them on the sofa.

"Please, think about having a nap, darling," Constance said. She kissed Carter, waved goodbye and then left the office, closing the door behind her.

Constance Osterman and Carter Wilkins? How the hell had that happened?

Carter must've seen my question on my face.

"We met because I kept going to the library to do research and look into all those old papers that Ollie and you had been sorting. We hit it off and here we are," Carter said and then gave a gigantic yawn.

I wasn't quite sure what to say. I'd never considered that Carter had a personal life. Most of the time to me he was just this annoying person who lived in Harlot Bay who wrote lies about my family in the newspaper or who would jump out at any random occasion and wave a digital recorder in my face. I guess it was a lot easier to hate someone if you didn't know any personal details about them. Maybe I'd avoided learning anything about him because knowledge led to empathy and I wouldn't be able to safely hate him from a distance.

I didn't want to say congratulations because that felt wrong so I waved to the boxes instead. "So what's all this?" I asked.

"It's research on August and Sylvester Coldwell and their family. I copied every file that I've gathered, every piece of information, and I'm bringing it here. I want you to go through it, extract out of it what you can and then we'll compare notes. I think if we work together we can prove beyond a shadow of a doubt that August and Sylvester Coldwell are complicit in crimes and they come from a family that has committed many crimes, and then we'll be able to shut the mall project down and hopefully send both of them to prison for a very long time," Carter said.

I went over to one of the boxes and took a quick look at one of the files. It was property sales records from the 1980s. I saw the name Anthony Coldwell appear on the papers. He was Sylvester and August's father.

I saw Carter yawn again and I caught it. I gave an enormous yawn and then slipped the file back into the box.

"Sure, I'll look through it, but this is going take a long time," I said.

"Go as fast as you can. I think they're behind the sabotage in town and I don't think they're going to stop until someone stops them, so you have a direct interest here," he said.

I remembered that yesterday he'd sent me a message saying *You need to urgently talk to me.*

"You needed to talk to me yesterday? What about?" I asked.

"Oh, it was nothing. Don't worry about it," Carter said, looking away. He walked over to my desk, picked up a piece of paper and wrote on it before handing it to me.

Your office may be bugged.

"Okay, well, thanks for bringing me these files. I'll be sure to keep them safe," I said.

I was playing along but part of me thought that maybe Carter was going crazy, probably from the sleep deprivation he was clearly suffering. I couldn't ask him about that either, but I guessed he'd been out doing surveillance of some kind or the other. If he thought the room was bugged why did he talk so openly about the Coldwells just now?

"Oh, I think you need to publish your article too about the sabotage. Finish writing it up and send me a copy but then I think we'll be good to go," Carter said. With that he said goodbye and then he was gone, leaving me in my office, looking around wondering if I would know what a bug looked like if I saw it.

I spent all of five minutes briefly flicking through the

files. There was simply a ridiculous amount of information in them. Sales records, newspaper articles, Health Department records. It appeared to me that since Carter had been evicted from his office location by Sylvester Coldwell all that time ago that he developed somewhat of a fixation and had spent the intervening time finding everything and anything he could about the Coldwell family. I even found copies of paperwork going back over a hundred years where some great-great-grandfather had bought an orchard after a fire had occurred and then had sold it many years later for a great profit. I recognized that paperwork—me and Ollie had found it in the archives under the library long ago.

I set the files aside, briefly wondering whether I should leave them up in the office where they could easily be stolen or whether I should take them home and hide them somewhere in the mansion. I returned to my laptop and started looking into Morris Sanderson, the night security guard who'd been killed. As a man in his fifties, there weren't many traces of him online given that he'd grown up in the era before the Internet. I did find a few things however, and they directly connected Sylvester and Morris together. I found a photo of Sylvester twenty years ago, looking young and much slimmer, Standing to his side in a black tuxedo was Morris. In the photo caption he was described as Sylvester's bodyguard. I found one other article from the deeper past that had been recovered from the Harlot Bay library's scanning efforts. A local basketball team of sixteen-year-olds were to travel to a nearby town to play their rivals, The Hawks. Listed in the team were Sylvester Coldwell and Morris Sanderson. In the photo of the team two grinning boys had their arms flung around each other. Morris was unrecognizable and honestly, so was Sylvester. I think it was the pure joy coming from a teenager's face. I'd never seen Coldwell look like that.

I was staring and thinking when I heard another rap on the door.

Oh my Goddess, it was a day for visitors.

"Who is it?" I called out. John Smith floated through the door and smiled at me.

"Oh, hey, John," I said. It was unusual for him to knock. Most of the time he just floated through or I would often find him in my office watching television when I got there.

"Hi, Harlow, may I watch television? My favorite court show's about to start," he said.

"Sure, not a problem, I'll get it for you," I said. I turned on the television. It was on the infomercial channel that John usually favored. This time they were selling a glamorized tent that came with all the modern conveniences of a home.

"It's glamping! It's *way* better than camping. Call now," the smiling host who was wearing too much fake tan said.

"I used to love camping," John said settling down on top of one of the boxes of files like it was a chair.

I changed the channel until I came to one where a courtroom drama was just beginning. I guess I was a bit distracted because I didn't get too excited about the fact that John had spoken about his past. Inevitably, if I questioned him about it he would forget he'd said anything at all. I returned to my computer and continued scrolling along through bits of information.

"Where did you used to go camping?" I asked John not really expecting an answer.

"Truer Island was always the best. There are even two waterfalls out there, within walking distance of the ferry. Of course you can keep going further into the heart of Truer Island and there is a small lake, and some caves with stalactites. I used to love going out there with my girlfriend," he said.

Okay, so he'd give me more of an answer than he'd ever given in the past. But that was no reason to get excited. Trying to keep any tone out of my voice, I carefully asked my next question. "Do you remember who you used to go camping with, John?" I asked. I continued scrolling through information on August Coldwell. It felt a little absurd, but I seemed to believe that if I didn't look directly at John or really think too hard about what he was saying, he might actually give me an answer.

"Jack," he murmured focused on the television.

"Jack? What?" I said.

"My name is Jack, not John," he said.

I suddenly couldn't breathe. I felt if I moved a muscle he'd forget everything.

"What is your last name Jack?" I asked.

John didn't respond but rather used his ghostly fingers to turn up the volume on the television. There had been a break in his legal drama for a local short news report.

"City police are still searching for the attacker behind the arson attack on the *Chili Challenge* warehouse. Sheriff Hardy has called for any witnesses to please ring the police station and give information. He has advised that people can remain anonymous if they wish to do so. In other news..." the reporter said.

"Oh, I know who did that," John said, pointing at the screen.

I finally had to pull myself away from my laptop. It seemed like John—or was his name Jack?—was in a talkative mood.

"Who firebombed the *Chili Challenge*?" I asked.

"I don't know his name, but I saw him, and I know where he lives," John said. "Quick come with me, I'll show you," he said. Before I could say anything, John glided out through the door, heading down the stairs. I called out to him to wait then bolted myself, following him down the stairs and out into the street.

I got a few strange looks from tourists and locals as I rushed down the street. I couldn't call out to John to slow down and soon I was jogging just trying to keep up. It wasn't long before I was sweating. Thankfully we didn't have to go too far. Just on the outskirts of what you would laughingly call the central business district of Harlot Bay was an old pub, probably one of the dodgiest and low-class ones that Harlot Bay had to offer. Behind it was a row of holiday rentals that were fairly gross and rundown. John finally came to a stop out on the street. I finally caught up to him and stopped myself, my hands on my knees trying to catch my breath.

"He went into number three. He was blond and a bit chunky with spiky hair. He was definitely the one," John said.

I was just starting to catch my breath and about to ask John what his last name was again when a car swept by and hit him.

Don't worry—John was fine, he's a ghost, but he bounced off the car like he'd been shot out of a cannon. The last I saw of him he was vanishing into the distance up the road, the sound of his surprised yell echoing away. The car that had hit him continued on unaware.

Despite my shock at seeing John propelled off into the distance my wits returned and I realized it wasn't a good idea to be standing out in the open in front of a building that possibly a suspected arsonist lived in or was renting. I crossed the road and found some trees and small bushes. I slipped in behind them and sat down to wait. It was a good thing I moved because about a minute later the front door of unit three opened and out came a pudgy blond man with spiked hair, just as John had described. Following close behind him was a darker-haired man who was tall, but looked solid. They got into what was obviously a rental car and then drove away down the street heading towards town. As soon as they were a little down the street, I started jogging down the road, hoping that all the tourist traffic would slow them down somewhat so wouldn't lose them. I needn't have worried about them disappearing though. As soon as we got to town, they slowed, driving around until they went down the road where *Traveler* and *The Cozy Cat* were. They parked on the other side of the road and then sat there. I found myself lurking in some shade by the side of the building watching the two men in their car. Were they watching *The Cozy Cat* and *Traveler*?

It seemed an odd place to park for no reason. My suspicion over their actions increased immensely the next moment when the blond man lifted up a pair of binoculars and looked across the road. I saw Luce and the health inspector come out of *Traveler*. The health inspector handed Luce something and then she triumphantly tore the giant orange sticker off the front window.

I looked back to the car with the two men in it. They were talking and soon after that started the car and drove away, heading out of town.

I jogged down the road, already sweaty enough that it didn't matter much now until I reached *Traveler*. Luce had gone back inside but had left the door unlocked. The bell above it jingled as I entered. My cousins were inside, and they had music playing, Luce doing some sort of dance in front of the counter and Molly behind it, singing away as she polished the front of the coffee machine.

"Harlow! We passed our inspection, we're ready to open again!" Luce said and came grabbed me in an enormous hug. I was incredibly happy for them, and their joy was infectious, but it wasn't enough to wipe away the worry that I was carrying along. Molly saw my face and switched the music off.

"What's wrong?" she asked.

"I think I found the thugs who sabotaged you and… they were just watching you from across the street. I think they might be going to do it again," I said.

CHAPTER TEN

We were going to be late for our big family dinner if we didn't hurry up. Molly was standing half-dressed in the kitchen in the middle of freakout number six. Or maybe it was still the *original* freak out from when I told her and Luce this afternoon that I thought I'd discovered the two men who had attacked the *Chili Challenge* and were likely behind the sabotage of *Traveler* and the *Torrent Mansion Bed and Breakfast*.

"All I'm saying is they could be at *Traveler* right now stealing the coffee machine, and then we're ruined," Molly said, pointing a shoe at me.

"You have security cameras, Stefano is bolted down, and besides, I already told Sheriff Hardy, and I'm sure he's on the case. As soon as he finds them he'll investigate and hopefully take them off the streets," I said.

"That's not going to do us any good if they steal our coffee machine," Luce said. She at least was dressed.

"Can you please just get dressed and we'll go down to dinner and ask Sheriff Hardy. I know you're waiting on getting some alarms but maybe Jack can figure out something sooner," I said.

Molly stomped off to her bedroom and then returned with the rest of her clothes to continue getting dressed.

"What we need is a guard until we get the alarms connected," Luce said her arms crossed, biting her lower lip. She was looking around, not in the midst of a freak out herself, but sometimes dipping in and out of it when she felt like joining Molly. Her gaze came to rest on the sleeping Adams who was over on the sofa with Hugo snoring beside him. On the other sofa was Adams's girlfriend, or so we thought, Butterscotch, sound asleep.

"Adams can do it! He can stay over there and if someone breaks in he can come straight back here and get us," Luce said.

Adams woke up and blearily looked over. "I'm going to do what?" he asked and then yawned, showing his sharp white teeth.

"You can guard *Traveler*. Maybe you and Hugo can go over there and stay the night until we can get some proper alarms set up." Luce said. Adams stood up and stretched but then sat back down started giving himself a bath. I recognized the look on my sneaky cat's face. He was getting ready to try to make a deal.

"I think I'm going to need to be paid," Adams said, nibbling on his paw.

"How about you do it to pay us back, for eating all of our food and drinking our wine," I said.

Although I'd been extremely angry the other day when we discovered the chaos and ruin of Adams and Hugo eating and biting all of our food, it turned out it's extremely difficult to punish a cat and a mouse. You couldn't exactly send a cat to its room because it would just go to sleep, and the mouse didn't care either. We had to settle for a severe telling off, warning them both never to do it again. It seems Hugo had learned well from Adams and had completely denied that he'd been involved whatsoever even though we'd caught he and Adams at the scene of the crime.

"I didn't do that. I need to be paid. I have a girlfriend to support you know," Adams said. Over on the other sofa Butterscotch let out a sigh but continued sleeping.

"Just offer them something," Molly said, pulling on a pair of pantyhose.

"I'll give you a tin of tuna in the morning if you stay there all night," Luce said.

"A hundred tins of tuna," Adams demanded.

"You are out of your feline mind if you think you're going to get a hundred tins of tuna. I'll go and do it for one tin of tuna," I said, bluffing. Adams looked alarmed at the idea of losing even a single tin of tuna. He nudged Hugo awake with his paw. "We'll do it, a tin of tuna paid in the morning. Come on Hugo," he said. Without saying a word, Hugo leaped up onto Adams's back. Adams jumped over the back of the sofa, but we didn't hear him land.

My phone chimed in my pocket. A moment later, so did Molly and Luce's. We didn't need to look to know what it was: the Moms warning us against being late. On top of everything else, we didn't need a bunch of upset Moms to deal with so we hustled out of there, leaving Butterscotch asleep on the sofa.

We reached the mansion just as Sheriff Hardy arrived. We went inside to find the table was almost full already. Will and Ollie were there as was Jack. Aunt Cass was sitting at the head of the table, filling up glasses of wine, and Peta and Jonas were already drinking and talking. The Moms were hurrying in and out, and from the kitchen we could hear a lot of clanging.

"That was a close call," Jack commented, pointing his

finger at the clock.

Mom came bustling out of the kitchen carrying plates. She shoved them into my arms. "Oh good, you're finally here, set these out," she said and then spun about-face to race back to the kitchen.

"We're on time you know!" I called out to her back.

I laid out the plates and then went over to where Luce and Molly were talking with Sheriff Hardy in the corner.

"They're gone, Harlow," Luce said, dramatically. I looked at Sheriff Hardy, and he nodded.

"We went to that unit but it was empty. We followed it up with the rental agency but it was rented under fake names. I think maybe those two men saw you possibly," Sheriff Hardy said in a quiet voice.

This was evidently not what Molly wanted to hear and she moved on to freak out number seven. Thankfully Aunt Cass was nearby with a glass of wine. She shoved it into Molly's hand.

"Drink that and quit your panicking," she said. Thankfully Molly obeyed and then went back to sit next to her boyfriend, who put his arm around her.

"We're going to keep looking for them, Harlow, I promise," Sheriff Hardy said. We couldn't talk anymore because dinner was served and woe betide anyone caught out of their seat during dinner service. Tonight the Moms had gone on a traditional theme: roast chicken, roast potatoes, green beans, carrots, butter on everything, and plenty of glasses of wine.

I sat down beside Jack and squeezed his hand. I'd already taken a few sips of wine, and they'd headed straight to my stomach and my head and helped lift away some of the worries of the day and, frankly, of the week. As the food was served out and everyone was talking a mile a minute, Molly leaned over and whispered in my ear. "I'm just worried about Ollie seeing too much witchiness, and I don't want anything to happen to him if he is investigating that map," she said. She'd mentioned her worries briefly before, but we hadn't had a chance to talk about them properly.

The dinner tonight was to celebrate *Traveler* and the bed-and-breakfast both being able to reopen, but it also gave Aunt Cass a reason to pull Ollie into her investigation of the map that we'd discovered. If there was anyone who could decipher the locations and what they might possibly mean, it was Ollie, Harlot Bay's resident superstar librarian. Molly had grudgingly given her permission for him to be involved given that it was incredibly important that we discover what had happened in the past. But things like being transported naked out to the top of the Harlot Bay lighthouse had started to grow a great doubt in her mind as to whether Ollie would continue to stick around if things like that kept happening. There was also the very real worry about whether he would be safe.

I patted Molly's hand and then topped up her glass of wine. "It's just a bit of research, he'll be fine," I said. Molly took another sip of wine and then leaned back in her chair. We all started eating, the conversation going a thousand places at once. Jonas and Jack talked about the Governor's mansion. The renovation was almost complete. Jonas was planning a grand opening and apparently had been in talks with the Mayor to host a gigantic Ball out there.

"So what are you going to do after that, builder man?" Aunt Cass asked.

"I'm sure I'll find something to do. Maybe I'll finish renovating my house plus Jonas has his eye on a few other places that we can fix up," Jack said.

"Maybe you should be using some of that Governor's mansion money to buy an engagement ring," Aunt Cass said. She'd taken a drumstick and was waving it around as she spoke.

"Aunt Cass! Let them be," Molly said.

But Aunt Cass was not to be deterred. "You've got to grab love while you can. It's important," she said, pointing the drumstick at Jack.

"That's great advice Cass thanks," he said, giving her a grin.

We changed topics after that, none of us witch cousins wishing to talk about marriage or what the next inevitable topic would be, which was babies. My cousins were extremely happy that the orange sticker was gone from the front of *Traveler* and so was Peta. They knew that business would likely be down when they reopened, but also I was going to be publishing the article about the sabotage in they hoped that that would turn things around. The Torrent Mansion Bed and Breakfast wasn't doing very well either. The Moms had lost all their bookings for the next month ahead and the online reviews now said that they'd been closed by the Health Department. But still they were upbeat. The Big Pie Bakery was still bringing in a lot of money and the construction was continuing apace on rebuilding the original Big Pie Bakery. It was almost complete and at the point of having the giant bakery ovens installed.

We talked and ate our way through dinner and then moved on to a delicious chocolate pudding with cream for dessert. After that I was sent off to the lounge to get the movie set up.

I'd used the code that Bella had given me to download *Witch Magic*. While I was in there Aunt Cass brought Ollie in and handed the map over to him, as well as the journal that we'd found. Ollie could hardly believe his eyes and was beside himself with excitement. I saw him glance across at the television with a disappointed look on his face.

"You know, you don't have to stay. It's just a movie," I said to him.

"It's a movie that Molly's in and the rest of you too. It's important," Ollie said, although his voice trailed away a bit at the end as he started flipping through the journal. Aunt Cass then did him a favor and took the map and journal from him telling him she would return it to him at the end of the night. Then she called everyone to the lounge. We brought in extra chairs to fit everyone and more bottles of wine.

I settled in next to Jack on the sofa as the opening credits of *Witch Magic* played on the screen. I felt a small tug of sadness in my heart when I saw that the film had been dedicated to Matthias Matterhorn who had sadly died during production. He'd been murdered, something that the Hollywood press had made much mileage from in regard to the release of the movie. Soon we were watching Bella Bing on the screen, a carefree girl living in a small town who was about to discover she was a witch. Molly snorted at something Bella said but even she couldn't keep it up for long. Bella was annoying, incredibly so, but she actually was a decent actor and soon we were lost in the story.

As we watched, Jack occasionally spoke, mentioning bits of the scenery that he'd worked on. The night carried on with all of us sipping wine and watching. It was getting late, the movie heading towards its conclusion, Bella Bing as her witch character about to solve the mystery, and we still hadn't seen the scenes that we had filmed. Bella had virtually threatened the director with walking off the set if he didn't put us in as some extras, and I'd even had a line saying, "It's fabulous, darling". Aunt Cass had been in the film as well.

"It's nearly over. Where are we?" Aunt Cass said.

The film finished a few minutes later, the end credits rolling up the screen.

"We were cut! They cut us!" Aunt Cass said, stomping about the room.

"Typical Bella. I bet you it was *her*," Molly said.

I was feeling far too relaxed to get into it. "Things get cut out of films all the time," I said, trying to be the voice of reason.

"I told people I was going to be in that. They've killed my Hollywood career by cutting me out of that film," Aunt Cass said, hitting the heights of dramatic performance. I remembered Bella sitting in *The Cozy Cat* after handing over the code for the movie. She'd said something about us all being wonderful in it. Clearly she'd known we'd all been cut from the film.

The night finished after that. Sheriff Hardy and Aunt Ro heading on their way back to their home and me, Molly and Luce reluctantly kissing our respective boyfriends goodbye. We did all want them to stay with us, but given we simultaneously had no magic and slip magic at once it definitely wasn't safe. I certainly didn't want to end up on the top of that lighthouse with Jack in our bed. I gave Jack a kiss before he jumped in his truck and headed away down the hill. As we wandered back to our end of the mansion through the warm night air we chatted a bit about the upcoming school reunion.

"I am *so* going to find a way to spill a drink on Bella Bing," Molly declared.

"Maybe we should let bygones be bygones and just try to have a good time," Luce said.

"No way, Torrent. She knew that we'd been cut from that. She probably even had a hand in it. I would be willing to let bygones be bygones if they really *were* bygones. But they're not bygones, they're *rightnows*, and she keeps doing things. There is no way I'm going to let her outshine us at that reunion," Molly said. We went inside, where Butterscotch was still sleeping soundly on the sofa. I brushed my teeth and then crashed into bed in the warm embrace of a good dinner, good times, and a few glasses of white wine.

CHAPTER ELEVEN

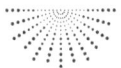

My blissful sleep was broken by the sound of muffled whispering from the kitchen.

Urgh, what time was it? My phone helpfully told me it was one am. I stumbled out to the kitchen and flicked the light on to find Molly and Luce in complete camouflage gear, wearing black balaclavas. Molly had her phone out with the light on using it to try to apply camouflage make-up around her eyes.

"What are you two doing?" I said, rubbing my eyes.

"Nothing, we're not doing anything," Molly said.

"Yeah, can't two witches just wear camouflage gear in their own house," Luce said. I stared at them until they broke.

"Okay, fine. We're gonna sneak unto Coldwell's office and see what we can find," Molly said.

I rolled my eyes and tried to get my brain to work. "But why would you do that?" I asked.

"Because Coldwell's got guys watching *Traveler* setting up to sabotage it again and so we're going to take the fight to him," Luce said. As she spoke she picked up Aunt Cass's crowbar from the table and started swinging it around for emphasis.

"Isn't it safer just to put a guard on *Traveler* or an alarm and then see if Sheriff Hardy can catch those guys?"

"Oh sweet Harlow, you're so innocent," Molly said.

"Like a little fawn in the forest," Luce added, pulling up her balaclava just to smirk at me.

I stood there for a moment, pondering whether I should go back to bed before I decided not to.

"Okay, fine, but I'm coming with you. First all you need to get out of those ridiculous camouflage clothes. Bring the balaclavas for when we get into the place. But you need to dress in ordinary clothes. There's probably still tourists around and we need to blend in," I said.

Molly stopped smearing camouflage make-up around her eyes.

"That's actually a good idea," she said. She headed off to her bedroom to get changed.

"Why didn't you tell me about this?" I asked Luce. She pulled her balaclava off and dropped it on the table, placing Aunt Cass's crowbar next to it.

"Well, you're reporting on it and we didn't want you to get involved because if we get caught it's going to destroy your credibility and we need it," Luce said.

"You don't think it's going to destroy my credibility that my two cousins who I live with get arrested?" I asked.

"We're not gonna get arrested. I looked up on the Internet how to disable alarms, we'll be fine," Luce said.

I rolled my eyes at this and went back to my room to change. The night was still warm. I put on a pair of dark shorts and a dark top, and black shoes. By the time I came back out to the kitchen Molly and Luce had both changed, and Molly had wiped most of the makeup off her face.

"I think this is a bad idea but let's go," I said.

Soon we were in Molly's car heading down the hill, sipping away on the instant coffee that Luce had insisted on making before we went. I was fully awake now and sliding between *okay, this might be a good idea* and *we're gonna get caught, we're gonna go to jail.*

"We'll park a few doors away from Coldwell and then come in the back entrance," Molly said, taking a sip of coffee.

"What is it you think you're gonna find there?" I asked.

"I don't know. But I want to go and look. If he's gonna steal our coffee machine and sabotage the shop, then I'm gonna break into his office and see what he's up to," Molly said.

I didn't say anything to that. I highly doubted Coldwell would be stupid enough to leave papers around his office implicating him in anything, but I also knew I wouldn't be able to stop my cousins by pointing this out. After all it had been their coffee shop that had been sabotaged and I'd seen the two thugs across the road watching it. Not to mention their coffee machine had been stolen in the past a long time ago and had destroyed their business until it had been returned.

Soon we were in town and had parked in a darkened alleyway two streets away from where Coldwell's office was. Molly had a slim small black bag into which she had slipped Aunt Cass's crowbar.

We crept through the night not seeing anyone else out on the streets and it wasn't long before we were standing at the back door of Coldwell's office. Luce went over to the power box and opened it up.

"Please don't electrocute yourself," I said.

"I told you, Harlow. I looked it up on the Internet," Luce said, as though that was some great source of authority.

I thought she was going to do some high-tech wizardry with bits of wire but all she did was flick the power off. Then she came back over to the door, opened Molly's bag and pulled out a lockpick.

"How did you learn to do that?" I asked.

"Jack showed me," Luce said. A moment later, there was a click as the door unlocked and Luce slipped the lockpick into her pocket.

"I think sometimes our family should just become outright criminals. We may as well the amount of breaking into places we do," I muttered, following my cousins inside.

We stopped for a moment to put on our balaclavas to cover our faces and Molly handed out pairs of dishwashing gloves from her bag. It might have looked ridiculous but it would stop us getting our fingerprints on anything. She passed out flashlights but warned us to be careful with them because anyone seeing lights flickering through the front window would be very suspicious.

In Coldwell's office it was warm, the air-conditioning off at night. We checked the front reception desk and found nothing but paper and pens and other bits of stationery. We then went out through some doors and found a row of filing cabinets that were all unlocked.

"Just more contracts," Luce commented after we spent a quick ten minutes searching through them. They were just sales contracts of various properties that Coldwell had been involved in. It appeared he'd also been involved in the sale of other properties as well, acting as a real estate agent.

"I wish we'd brought a whole heap of dirt and grease and mouse droppings so we could dump it in here," Luce muttered as we shut the filing cabinets.

"Wouldn't that make it super obvious to Sheriff Hardy that it was us considering we reported that happening to *us*?" I asked.

"Maybe the saboteur has a M.O. They're just doing what

they do," Luce said. We made our way out to Coldwell's office.

We searched Coldwell's office. There was a small cabinet of papers in there but they just turned out to be more real estate transaction documents. Luce used her lockpick on the drawer in his desk and that's where we hit pay dirt. She pulled out a thick file and opened it, only to be confronted by her own face and a list of facts.

"He has us in here," Luce whispered. She flipped the page to show a photograph of Molly and then one of me. The small folder was full of information on people in the town. There were pages on the Mayor, some on council members, there was one on Jack, Sheriff Hardy, our Moms, and other random people in the town. I grabbed my file and started reading. I was listed as a journalist/novelist. All the jobs I'd had were listed, including working at the Big Pie Bakery and my part-time jobs over the years. It looked like Coldwell had been compiling this information for at least the last two or three years. There was even a page in there about the event that had sent me returning to Harlot Bay when there'd been a fire at the apartment block where I'd been staying. I'd gone to bed with Adams curled up on my toes and woken to the sounds of fire sirens. I'd gotten out of there with Adams, my laptop and the clothes on my back. No one had died but the fire consumed the building and that had been the final straw. I'd got in my car and returned home.

All three of us were engrossed in our files when we started at the sound of a large thud from the other room.

"What was that?" Molly said, her eyes wide in the dark.

There were more thuds and the sound of something being knocked over.

"Someone's here," Luce whispered. She reached into the bag and pulled out Aunt Cass's crowbar, holding it like a weapon.

"Put that away, if you hit someone with that you could kill them," I whispered. The thudding from the other room grew in volume. But it wasn't footsteps, or a person. It sounded like someone was out there, throwing a tennis ball around at high speed. I put my file down, went to the door and carefully opened it. As soon as I did something whizzed past my head, hit the back wall and burst into pieces.

"Someone is throwing something!" I said. There was a thud from behind me and Molly squealed as something bounced off her head and landed on Coldwell's desk. Luce turned her flashlight onto it.

It was a cinnamon donut.

"Oh Goddess, it's the flowers all over again but it is donuts," Luce moaned. I hit the light switch on the wall and lit up Coldwell's office. I saw a donut materialize out of nothing, and fling across and hit Luce on the shoulder. It broke into pieces and fell to the ground. Two more donuts appeared out of nowhere, traveling at high speed. One hit a framed painting on the wall, knocking it down. The glass shattered as the painting hit the floor. The other donut hit the blinds behind Coldwell's desk, breaking them.

"We need to get out of here right now," Molly said.

There was no argument from either of us. Luce grabbed the files and we bolted. Out in the main room of Coldwell's office the chaos was far worse than I could have imagined. The entire office was at least ankle deep in donuts, all cinnamon. Donuts were appearing out of the air, flinging all over the place. More of the framed paintings on the walls had been hit and had fallen down. We rushed out of his office, leaving the door open behind us and fled into the darkness. I was nursing a small hope that as we ran, we would leave the donut storm behind us, but it simply followed us along through the dark.

"We need to find somewhere to hide out!" I yelled. It

crossed my mind that perhaps it was only one of us responsible for this and if we split up maybe we could find out who it was. But what use was that? There were still donuts appearing from nowhere, flinging all over the place. There was a loud clattering sound as a flurry of donuts knocked the lids off some steel trashcans in an alleyway. We reached Molly's car and leaped inside. We slammed the doors shut and Molly roared off. We quickly realized our serious mistake. Whatever this magic was, it seemed to constrain itself to any enclosed space that we were in. The speed of donuts appearing out of the air quickened but they were all inside the car. We wound the windows down but it wasn't much use. Donuts were hitting the windshield and us as well.

"We have to stop," Molly squealed as a particularly fast donut hit her in the back of the head. We were speeding out of town, but I realized it wasn't in the direction of our home. We were on a dark road being pelted with donuts when I saw the lighthouse ahead of us.

"In there, in there," I called out. Molly skidded to a stop in the car park and we bolted out. We couldn't stay in the open and be pelted by donuts so we rushed up to the lighthouse and went inside. Normally it was chained shut to keep local teenagers out and other inquisitive folk but we'd been up here so many times recently that on one of our previous trips we'd simply cut the chain so we could get inside. We entered the lighthouse and tried to find a corner to barricade ourselves in. There were old building materials left down there, bits of sheet metal and wire from when someone had been renovating the lighthouse, trying to bring it back to life. We grabbed some of the sheet metal and made ourselves an impromptu cave against the wall. It was there we hid for the next hour as donuts continued appearing out of nowhere and pelting our shelter. Eventually it came to an end and we crawled out. The bottom of the lighthouse was more than knee deep in donuts, all cinnamon.

"You know what, I'm having one," Luce said.

"They're magic though, who knows what's in them," I said but that didn't stop her. She picked up one from the top of the pile and took a bite, then groaned in pleasure.

"They're really good," she said through a mouthful.

Oh Goddess, why not? I ate a cinnamon donut and so did Molly and then we made our way back to the car. It took us a few minutes to clean the donuts out before we could get inside. The entire inside of the car smelled like cinnamon and sugar. I was sure there were probably a few donuts hidden under the seat somewhere.

"We have to get home before anyone sees us. There is no way we're gonna be able to hide all those donuts," Luce said.

I had to reluctantly agree. We would need a few trucks and an army of volunteers to clean out the lighthouse. Not to mention there was a trail of donuts spread through Harlot Bay leading back to Coldwell's office.

We drove back into town, Molly trying to keeping to side streets so no one would see us, and soon we were heading out the other side on our way home. Luce and I had split Coldwell's file in half and we were both looking through it. Luce found a file that had a small photo on it and showed it to me, shining a flashlight on it. It was the blond man, chubby with spiky hair. The name on the paper said Clifford Pascoe.

"That's definitely the guy," I said. Clifford's sheet was actually a rap sheet of various crimes he'd been involved in over the years: arson; theft; breaking and entering. He'd served some prison time too, up until about a decade ago when he'd gone clean, or perhaps stopped being caught.

"Is it just me or is Clifford Pascoe the wrong name for a thug?" Luce commented.

"Keep looking, see if the other one is in there," I said. I checked the rest of my papers, but the other man wasn't in there. Luce found him however. She passed me his file.

"Lazarus Walden," I said out loud and started to read. He'd been a criminal with a long history too until about ten years ago. It seemed his crimes had abruptly stopped and I was willing to bet all the money in the world that it was when he'd been hired by Coldwell.

"See, *that's* a hired goon name. Lazarus Walden. That's what you need in a goon. Not *Clifford*. He sounds like an accountant," Luce said.

We were soon home and inside. It was now past three in the morning and the coffee we'd drunk had worn off long ago. All of us were sticky and covered in cinnamon, but despite our tiredness we knew better than to just leave the files out in the open. Molly took them and hid them all up in the roof space. Then after a quick five-second argument about who got to use the shower first (resolved when I just jumped in there without bothering to argue about it), I took myself off to bed hearing the faint sound of the shower running as Molly washed the sugary sweetness off herself. Despite my tiredness I had a difficult time drifting away to sleep. Files of people just seemed super creepy and I didn't like it one bit that I discovered myself in there and the rest of my family. At least we had names now for the two goons that I'd seen and as soon as I got up in the morning I'd let Sheriff Hardy know so he could have a chance of tracking them down. By the time I went to sleep I'd almost completely forgotten that we had left Coldwell's office knee deep in donuts, a path of them through the town and then up to the lighthouse.

CHAPTER TWELVE

The morning saw three very tired and grumpy witches attempting to stay awake for breakfast to think through what had happened last night. We'd been up since six when Adams had returned from his guard duty and began meowing his head off like an idiot. He'd woken everyone up, calling out that he was starving hungry and then had come to my bedroom door to bang his paws on it. Despite the fact he was a magical cat, and could come and go from anywhere he wanted, it seemed that sometimes he forgot this and so he would bang on doors insisting on being let in or out. After I fed him I joined my cousins in the kitchen. It seemed that none of us had slept well. When I sat down at the table Molly blinked at me sleepily and looked me over.

"You have huge bags under your eyes," she commented.

"Yeah? Well so do you," I said, feeling a little bit annoyed.

"So do I. We all do. And the school reunion's tomorrow night!" Luce said.

Oh yeah, the school reunion. "Wait, are you sure? Is that tomorrow?" I said. I silently counted days in my head. Yup it was tomorrow all right. It had crept up faster than I expected.

"You can't go to the reunion looking like that," Molly said.

"I only look like this because you two insisted on going on a crime spree last night," I said.

"Correction—crime spree with a good result considering we found those files," Molly said. I grumbled something that perhaps could have been interpreted as "Okay you're right", and stumbled off to the kitchen to make some breakfast. I whipped up some bacon and eggs for everyone while Luce and Molly made coffees. Soon we were eating and once the food hit our stomachs, starting to feel little better.

"I don't think a night of sleep is going to get rid of these bags," Molly said, rubbing her eyes.

"That's what makeup is for," Luce said. The three of us were just starting to feel better when the front door slammed open and in came three witch mothers at high speed.

"Breaking and entering!" Mom yelled.

"How could you be so reckless?" Aunt Ro said.

"You are all grounded," Aunt Freya said, taking things a little bit too far.

"You can't ground us we're adults," Luce said to her mom.

"Do you know what the town is talking about this morning? Sylvester Coldwell's office is filled with donuts and then there is a trail of them through the town up to the lighthouse, which is knee deep in donuts," Mom said, turning slightly hysterical.

Okay, so Adams will lie in the face of direct evidence and being directly caught, but that cat had *nothing* on us witches.

"There are donuts in town?" Molly said innocently.

"Is that some sort of weird practical joke?" Luce asked.

"That *is* weird," I commented and took myself off to the kitchen, grabbing the plates as I went.

"Oh no, no, no, no, no, you can't get away with this. That

quantity of donuts is magic, unless of course someone went to all the bakeries and ran them for two or three days straight to cook them," Mom said, waggling a finger at the three of us.

"We really need to get to work," Luce said.

"No, you really need to pack your bags because you're going to have to go out to Truer Island and stay in the cave until this magical slip wears off," Aunt Ro said.

"We're not doing that. We have a school reunion to go to tomorrow," Molly said.

"Oh and what if flowers start falling from the ceiling or donuts or something else?" Aunt Freya said.

"Those flowers only turned up because one of us was stressed, that's all. And we don't know what you're talking about in regards to donuts," Molly lied.

"Besides, how do we know the donuts in town aren't from one of you three? You're the ones who own a bakery and you're kitchen witches," Luce said.

Ah, an excellent tactic! Go on the attack when yourself have been accused.

The argument might have gone on for much longer. The Moms were certainly angry enough for it but then Sheriff Hardy pulled up outside our end of the mansion. He stepped out of his police car and we saw he was wearing his stone face cop look. He came in without bothering to knock.

"Morning dear, aren't you meant to be at the bakery?" he said to Aunt Ro.

"Emergency family meeting, secret witch business," Aunt Ro lied.

Sheriff Hardy nodded and looked the six of us over. He could see that me, Molly and Luce were exhausted and had clearly stayed up late at night.

"There was a break-in last night at Sylvester Coldwell's office. It seems that in some kind of bizarre prank someone dumped thousands of cinnamon donuts there, including in his office after vandalizing the place. Then they spread a trail of donuts through town up to the old lighthouse, which they filled with donuts again. Do any of you know anything about this?" he said.

"Donuts? That's strange," Mom said.

"Donuts in his office? That does sound weird," Aunt Freya added.

"Where would somebody even get that many donuts?" Aunt Ro said.

Ah the Moms. They could lie with the best of them.

Sheriff Hardy knew when he was being stonewalled.

"The good thing is, it looks like some kind of incredibly bizarre prank. Hopefully it won't happen again, or perhaps the people doing it might take themselves somewhere safe so it doesn't happen again," he said.

"Anyway, we need to get back to the bakery," Aunt Ro said. She kissed Sheriff Hardy on the cheek and fled out of there with Aunt Freya close behind her. Mom said her goodbyes, heading for the other end of the mansion, although there were no guests for her to look after today. The three of them abandoned us, leaving me, Molly and Luce with Sheriff Hardy. Sometimes it was every witch for herself.

"We have to go to work too," Luce said. They vanished in an instant off to their bedrooms to get ready, leaving me standing there with Sheriff Hardy. I collected the dishes and focused on washing them so I wouldn't have to look at him.

"Some files were stolen from Sylvester Coldwell's yesterday. I wonder if they have anything interesting in them?" Sheriff Hardy commented.

He knew, we knew, but none of us was going to say it. So it was time for another lie.

"Just on a different topic, I checked with some sources last night and I've come up with some names of those two men. One is called Clifford Pascoe, he's the blond one with spiky hair. The other one is called Lazarus Waldron. They both have long criminal records," I said.

Sheriff Hardy dutifully wrote down the names.

"That's great work from your sources. Let's just hope that next time they find a better way to get that information," he said. He said goodbye and was soon on his way. As soon as he was gone, Molly and Luce emerged from their bedrooms. Both of them flopped down on the sofa.

"I am so tired. I do *not* want to go to work today," complained Luce.

"We have to even though there'll probably be no one there," Molly said.

I was debating whether I would simply crawl back into bed myself when Jack rang.

"Harlow, do you want to join me for a day of house renovation? We're nearly finished and I've got something special to show you," he said. I checked the time. It was still before seven.

I was still so tired I knew there was no way I was going to do any productive journalism work today. It seemed far better that I would spend some time with Jack.

"That sounds great. Can I come over about ten? I need to have a bit more sleep," I said.

"That'll be perfect. We can do some work and then have lunch out in the garden," Jack said. I told him I'd see him later and then hung up.

"You're taking the day off?" Molly said accusingly.

"Hey, I don't run a coffee shop. I'm just a journalist and a part-time one at that," I said. I left my two cousins grumbling as I took myself off to bed. Adams was already curled up at the end, asleep.

It seemed I'd only just laid down when my alarm on my phone was chirping at me. It was nearly ten already. I rushed out of bed, had a five-second shower and then drove into town and over to the house Jack was renovating. The day was beautifully warm but not too hot, a perfect temperature for doing some renovations.

Although I'd trooped in and out of Jack's house many times, it seemed today that entire house had stepped up a level, transforming from work-in-progress to almost complete. The front garden was looking beautiful and when I stepped into the entranceway, there was a beautiful light coming down from the window high above. The wooden floors were gleaming. Jack came rushing out of the back room and gave me a huge hug and a kiss. When he put me on the ground he then zipped off to the other room to return with a copy of the *Harlot Bay Times*. The front-page story was the donuts.

"Maybe we can talk about this while we work," Jack quipped.

"As I said to Sheriff Hardy and the Moms, I don't know anything about donuts," I said. Then I grinned and gave Jack another kiss. "Okay, but it's a ridiculous story."

We went off to the downstairs bathroom to clean up sanded bits of wood and then strip back a vanity unit before it could be painted. As we worked I talked to Jack about the previous night, what we had found in Coldwell's office, and then the flood of donuts that had attacked us. As I told the story Jack started laughing and I realized it was kind of funny. I don't know, maybe it was because I was tired and had only slightly recovered but the whole thing seemed more absurd than dangerous. It was lurking somewhere in the back of my mind that perhaps the Moms were right: we should go out to Truer Island and stay there. But I think I felt like Molly. I wanted to go to my school reunion. I didn't want to admit there was a problem. It wasn't long before we were approaching lunch and so we finished up and went to the kitchen to wash up. It was then Jack took me by the hand.

"I have something I want to show you," he said. He led me upstairs. Up at the top of the stairs was a writing room that a lifetime ago Jack had suggested could be mine. I guess in some imaginary future that we didn't really speak about we were married and living in this house. We'd even worked up in the writing studio on and off, but the last time I'd seen it, it had mostly been a mess and we'd moved onto more of the bottom rooms first. Jack pushed the door open and led me inside, and I let out a gasp. He must've been working on it in secret. There was a beautiful light shining in through the front window and there, in the middle of the room, was an old wooden desk and a chair. There was a corner lamp, which was currently off, and on two sides of the room there were bookcases polished light brown and empty. I took two steps into the room and then found myself crying. Jack grabbed me and kissed me.

"Why are you crying? Are these happy tears?" he asked.

I nodded and sniffed, my nose blocked. "They're very happy tears," I said.

"Check out this antique desk I got," Jack said, trying to distract me. He pulled me over to the middle of the room. The antique desk was old and weathered but it looked perfect.

"It's just the right size for a laptop if you want to do any writing, and I was thinking if you want to pick a spot for it maybe I could hide a power point somehow underneath it so there are no cords going across the room."

"It's perfectly beautiful," I said and then hugged him again.

Right in that moment of perfect silence my stomach grumbled aloud and we both laughed.

"Let's go out the back for a picnic," Jack said. We went downstairs back to the kitchen where I discovered that Jack had already prepared some food earlier. He had Vietnamese bread rolls, different cheeses, some olives, strawberries, some pepper crackers, grapes, and cold pale ale in the fridge. He put all of it onto an enormous dark brown chopping board. I carried the beers as I followed him outside and into the backyard. When he'd first bought the house the entire yard had been overgrown. It had been about two months ago when he'd finally hacked down all of the overgrown weeds and plants and discovered there was somewhat of a garden back there. There was even a beautiful lemon tree that was laden with fruit. Jack had dug up some of the yard and planted grass as well, which was now flourishing, dark green and lush.

We sat in the shade of the lemon tree and ate our lunch and drank our delicious cold beer. I looked over at Jack and saw he had bits of white paint in his hair and on his clothes. I looked down at myself and saw I had the same along with dirt and other smudges. Both of us looked a mess but he looked like a beautiful mess. His arms were strong and tanned, his hands were rough from working, and in the shade of a lemon tree, his eyes were a deep blue.

"Harlow, could you get me a lemon?" Jack asked. I stood up to retrieve the lemon from the tree and as I did Jack stood up too and came close to me. I pulled the lemon off just as Jack ducked down in front of me, reaching for his boot.

"Harlow Torrent, would you make me the happiest man in the world by…" he began.

I grinned at him and then dropped the lemon straight on his head.

"If you say by getting me a lemon I'm going to throw all of these at you," I said, laughing. The lemon bounced off Jack's head and rolled into the grass.

Jack laughed then reached into his pocket, and suddenly there was a ring in his hand.

"Instead of throwing a lemon at me, maybe you could marry me?" he said.

Let's be honest here, I'd imagined this moment many times, especially after Molly and Luce had gotten engaged. Sometimes I thought it might be on the beach. Other times as we sleepily lay next to each other in bed. I'd never thought that it would be out in the backyard of his house under a lemon tree with both of us covered in dirt and dust and paint, and just after I'd dropped a lemon on his head.

It's funny what perfection looks like. In your mind, you might think it's a suit and a perfect evening, but it turns out it's grass, the shade of a tree and your beloved covered in flakes of paint, looking up at you.

"Yes, I'll marry you," I said and then flung my arms around him, tumbling both of us to the ground.

Somewhere in there I ended up with an engagement ring on my finger and then we realized Jack had fallen onto the food and now had squished strawberries on his shirt. But that didn't matter, nor the dirt on our clothes or the bits of dried paint on our skin. We ended up underneath that lemon tree, breathing in the scent of the delicious citrus completely enraptured with each other.

CHAPTER THIRTEEN

"I can't breathe! Everyone get off me!"
"No, I don't know when the wedding is."
"Oh my Goddess, we are *not* talking about babies *now*!"

CHAPTER FOURTEEN

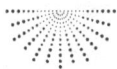

"Hieronymus Bosch," Molly said applying lipstick. "Isn't the entire point of a code word that you can say it as part of a normal conversation and it doesn't sound weird?" I said, checking my eyeshadow.

"I can say Hieronymus Bosch as a normal part of conversation. Look. 'I really enjoy the paintings of Hieronymus Bosch'," Molly said.

"How is that going to come up in general conversation? What conversation are you in where you can just say that?" I said.

"Harlow, it's a school reunion, people are going to be drinking, no one is going to care. I guarantee it," Molly said.

"I'm gonna say Salvador Dali," Luce said, checking her lipstick.

"No, we need to use the same code word so we remember what it is," Molly said.

"So change yours to Salvador Dali then," Luce said, shrugging.

"No, you change yours to Hieronymus Bosch."

"Look, it doesn't matter, just say whatever famous painter you want, we'll figure it out," I said.

It was the night of the high school reunion and we were getting ready while our assorted boyfriends waited in the lounge. Although all of us had made sure to go to bed early the previous night to catch up on sleep, we hadn't quite caught up enough to get rid of the bags under our eyes. Thankfully that's what make-up is for. We were all essentially wearing versions of the little black dress and I have to say, we were looking pretty good. I mean we had Moms who owned a bakery, so it was lucky that we were as slim as we were.

"Did you want to wear this necklace?" Luce asked me.

"You can have it, I have the only piece of jewelry that I really want," I said, flashing my engagement ring.

"Oh Goddess, I hope Bella Bing's there and says something mean to you about that. Then you can shove that in her face," Molly said.

We finished up in the bathroom and went out to the lounge. We were looking good but boy oh boy, our fiancés were looking even better. Will and Ollie had gone with the black pants pale blue shirt combinations. Ollie was wearing a slightly older style so he looked a little bit like a 19th Century paperboy but he had his shirt sleeves rolled up and his collar open, and looked amazing. Will had his sleeves rolled up too, showing his strong tanned arms. Jack had arrived in a pale blue suit with a light blue shirt underneath, and black pants. I have to say he was rocking that suit. All three of them had a bit of scruff, and slightly messy hair, and we three witches couldn't be happier about taking them to our reunion to show them off.

"Okay kids time to make an entrance," Molly said and grabbed Ollie. Luce grabbed Will and they rushed out the front door.

"We'll be right behind you," I said, remembering I'd forgotten my earrings. I rushed back to my room, found my earrings and put them on. By the time I came back to the lounge, Molly, Luce and their boyfriends were already driving off down the hill. Jack was waiting for me with a slight smile on his face.

"What are you so happy about?" I asked him.

"I'm just excited to see my fiancé," Jack said. We'd been doing this since we'd gotten engaged, trying out that new word *fiancé*. Yesterday after bringing him up to the mansion and then both of us nearly being crushed to death by the Moms and my cousins and Aunt Cass in hugs and kisses and a million questions, we'd had dinner, home-made and gone to bed early so I could catch up on sleep. Then Jack had gone to work all day trying to finish up the renovation on his house while I'd done nothing, trying to take a break from all the crazy things that were going on in my life. I was content to let Sheriff Hardy handle crime as that was actually his job. Throughout the day Jack and I'd kept messaging each other things about being engaged.

"Are we ready to go?" I asked.

"Do you think we're going to live together now that we're engaged?" Jack asked.

"I hadn't really thought about it, but I guess so," I said.

Both Molly and Luce were engaged but neither of them had officially moved out. All three of us were just spending more time *there* and less time *here*. I mean I already had a bunch of clothes over at Jack's house, a toothbrush and other things. I guess that's how it went: gradually we would move enough things over there until one day we would just decide it was official and the final move would be one small suitcase of clothing, if that.

"No pressure, but I would like to see you more than I do currently see you," Jack said, his eyes twinkling.

I was feeling happy, honestly, and after a day of rest all the chaos in Harlot Bay was the furthest thing from my mind. I was looking forward to the reunion and having fun, but suddenly a bolt of sadness went through me. Would Molly, Luce and I move out, marry our fiancés, have children and then suffer the same fate as the Moms? Eventually the magic would overwhelm our men and they would leave us, abandoning their families? Would we then return to live in Torrent Mansion as generations of witches had done before us? I shook my head, trying to remove that sudden bleak future and focused on Jack.

"I think we should move in with each other. What do you say about next week?" I asked.

Despite the fear of what may be you need to be brave and take a leap, even knowing that you may end up bruised at the end. Because although that is the risk, sometimes, just sometimes, you end up flying.

"I think that sounds great. I need someone to help me do more sanding at the house," Jack said and gave me a kiss.

We drove into town in his truck, talking a bit about people from high school who I thought might be there. Soon we reached the Harlot Bay High School. The reunion was in the hall where we'd had countless school assemblies. We could already hear the music from inside. Everyone attending tonight had bought a ticket which had helped rent the hall, hire caterers, pay for an open bar, a live band, and also hire some teenage waiters to ferry food and serve drinks. I knew that Sophira and Kira were working tonight as well as their boyfriends, Fox and Tony, together with a bunch of other teenagers. We parked in front of the high school and walked in through the gates. Nostalgia and the past were already hitting me. Although the school looked slightly different—trees were bigger or missing entirely and things had been painted—the bones of the school were just the same. I stopped Jack out the front of the hall and pointed to a red pole.

"First on our tour is a pole that I ran headfirst into when I was thirteen years old," I said.

"Fascinating," Jack said.

"Later on we'll go on a tour and you can see where I punched Abby Crookshank and where she punched me on a different occasion," I said narrating as though I was doing a nature documentary. Jack grabbed me by the arm and pulled me through the open doors of the hall.

Inside it looked simply magical. There were strings of fairy lights everywhere, and giant lanterns hanging from the lights above that gave the entire hall a warm dim glow. It was definitely mood lighting, the type that could hide crows feet and wrinkles and the fact that you might have put on a little bit of weight since high school. There were tables and chairs scattered about the place with small candles in glass jars in the center of them sending off a warm glow. There were already teenagers walking around wearing classic black and white, carrying platters of food. Over near the stage there was a dance floor with some people already on it dancing away. Over to one side was the open bar where people were already coming and going with glasses of wine and beer.

"I can't believe the place that we sat in and were so bored so many times looks this amazing," I said.

"Would you two crazy kids like a tiny sandwich?" Kira said suddenly from next to me.

"Ah! You need to wear a bell," I said nearly jumping out of my skin.

"Why would I do that? Then people would hear me when I wanted to be sneaky," the teenager said with a sly grin. She held her small platter of sandwiches out to us and we both took a tiny triangle. Mine was a simple ham and salad but it was quite delicious.

"Luce has already given me the word, so if you're in trouble just yell out Salvador Dali and I'll come and help," Kira said. Then she winked at us and zoomed away to offer sandwiches to another couple.

"Shall we go to the bar?" Jack asked.

"Absolutely," I said. It seemed everyone there had the same idea, heading directly to the bar when they first arrived. As we walked through the crowd everyone was looking at us and I couldn't help but look back in return. Some people I recognized . They looked like they'd barely changed. Others I'd no idea whether I'd gone to school with them or whether they were the partners of people I'd gone to school with. I saw a man smiling at me and he gave a little wave but I honestly had no idea who he was. Other people I could have spotted a mile off. I saw the three Belindas over near the side of the stage, laughing away and drinking glasses of wine. They had been best friends during high school and inseparable, and had gotten straight back together at the reunion. All three of them barely looked like they'd changed. I think if you put them in a school uniform they could have easily fit back in. We got to the bar and grabbed two glasses of wine. I wasn't feeling that nervous but perhaps I drank my wine a little quickly, just in case I was going to be nervous later on.

"So who shall we talk to first to dig up old wounds?" Jack said with a devilish grin.

"Or to have a good reminiscence," I said.

"That's boring. I want to hear juice, I want to hear problems. I would like to see a fight if I could," Jack said, looking around.

I scanned the crowd to see if there was anyone I could talk to.

"Hey, is that tall guy over there the one called Tom? Mr. super handsome football guy," Jack said. I looked in the direction was indicating. Yup it was Tom alright and I say this as a happily engaged woman who absolutely loves my fiancé, that Tom was looking simply spectacular wearing a slim-fitting dark blue suit.

"That's him," I said. Jack grabbed me by the arm and hauled me over, and suddenly we were in front of Tom. The girl he was talking to excused herself and disappeared into the crowd.

"See you later Julia," Tom called out. "Hey, Harlow, great to see you. Is this your amazing boyfriend?" he said, looking at Jack.

"He was my boyfriend the other day but actually we just got engaged so now he's my fiancé," I said.

"That's amazing. Congratulations," Tom said, and hugged the pair of us.

When he finally let us go he was grinning as though he'd heard the happiest news on earth that we were going to get married.

"So Harlow tells me that lots of girls had a crush on you in high school," Jack said, deciding to stir the pot.

I punched Jack in the shoulder as Tom laughed.

"Yeah… there were a few crushes going on and I feel sad I didn't tell them the truth back then but it was a secret I kept to myself," Tom said. He shouted out across the room, "Edward, Edward come here, meet some friends of mine," he said.

"Edward" may have had a very standard name but he was even better looking than Tom was. He had olive skin and green eyes, and was wearing a dark green well-fitted suit.

"Yes, my love?" Edward said to Tom once he arrived.

"This is Harlow and Jack, they're going to get married. It just happened," Tom explained.

"Congratulations, let's celebrate!" Edward said and waved one of the teenage waiters to bring some wine.

We got to talking while I digested this new piece of news, pieces of the puzzle falling into place and everything making sense. Every girl in high school had a crush on Tom but he hadn't had a crush on any of them and it wasn't because he was dedicated to football. I was lost in my memories thinking of the past and sipping on my second glass of wine, when I felt a finger tap me on the shoulder. I turned around and saw it was Bella Bing. Tom and Edward took that moment to excuse themselves to go meet other people. I saw Bella look Jack up and down and give him a sultry glance which, Goddess bless my boyfriend, he completely ignored. Then she focused her attention on me.

"Oh, Harlow, you look so tired," Bella said in a voice of fake concerned.

"I've just been working hard," I said.

"As a waitress you mean, at *The Cozy Cat*. Is that a hard job *working as a waitress?*" Bella said in a loud voice so people around us could hear.

"Bella did it upset you that the last film you were in only grossed thirty thousand and was panned as a universal failure?" Jack said .

"It's a cult classic," Bella said, and stormed away.

"Oh my Goddess, she is annoying," I said, trying to tell myself to stop clenching my wineglass lest it break in my hand.

"How about you take me for that tour right now?" Jack said. I decided that was an excellent idea. There were plenty of other people I saw looking at me, some of them bullies from the past and I knew they wanted to talk, but I was in no mood after running into Bella. I took Jack out a side door and soon we were walking around the school.

"Here is the spot where the famous punching of Abby Crookshank happened," I said, pointing to a patch of concrete, "And over there on the corner is where she punched me," I said.

"Any kisses had at this school?" Jack said, looking sideways at me.

"Actually now you mention it," I said and grabbed him by the hand. I led him around to the back of the school where there was a small grove of trees. The moon was out tonight and in its silvery gleam we could see the initials in love hearts carved into the bark of all the trees. I found the tree I was looking for and my initials.

"So who is this KM that you apparently love forever?" Jack asked, tracing his fingers over the carving.

"His name was Kyle Moretta. We were fourteen and deeply in love and then his parents moved away and I never saw him again," I said.

"Oooh, lost love. Well maybe he'll be here tonight and get another chance," Jack said.

"Nah I think I'll just leave him a burning flame in my heart," I said and poked him in the side. I crept around the back of the trees and looked around until I found what I was looking for. Because knives were forbidden at the school, of course, teenagers would hide them up near the trees so they could scratch initials where they wanted. I found a small pocketknife and got to work, scratching some new initials on the tree. I carved HT + JB in a love heart. And then stashed the pocketknife back where it had come from.

"There we go, now you're on the tree forever," I said. Jack stepped closer to me in the moonlight and took hold of my hands. "Now we're engaged I feel like I can tell you something deeply important to me," he said, his voice serious.

"What is it?" I asked.

"You should have carved JBB. My middle name is Bartholomew," he said.

"You're Jack *Bartholomew* Bishop? Oh my Goddess, how did I not know this?"

"I had to keep it secret till I had you in the bag. I even considered not telling you until we were married and had a baby, and you definitely couldn't go anywhere," he said.

"Hey, I'm not in the bag yet, I can take this ring off any time… Bartholomew," I said, laughing.

"What, you don't have some terrible middle name?" Jack said.

"Sorry, I don't have a secret like that for you. Witches don't do middle names. Although we *love* fake names. I sometimes get mail under the name Isabella Fantastic," I said. We headed back to the main hall joking and laughing and went back inside. We already had two drinks at least each so we made sure to start eating some food. The teenagers walking around would bring it over to your table if you sat down, so we sat to eat, having sandwiches, shrimp on skewers, little dumplings, and other bits and pieces. There were teenagers working everywhere with bottles of white wine and they would often refill your glass when it was half empty. It was getting very hard to track exactly how much we'd had to drink. We'd just finished eating and were heading for the dance floor, when Bella Bing appeared in front of me again.

"Harlow, did you see that Chester is here?" Bella said, pointing to the other side of the room.

Chester was a boy I'd gone out with for about four days back when I was fifteen years old. He was a sweet enough boy, but I wasn't for him and he wasn't for me. Now, ten years later he was a small portly man with thinning hair.

I could see what Bella was trying to do. Trying to make me feel bad about some boy I dated a million years ago. I saw Tom out on the dance floor dancing with some random girl and a plan formed.

"Oh my Goddess, Bella, did you see Tom from the football team? I was just talking to him before and it turns out he had a *huge* crush on me back in high school. I can't believe I never knew," I said. Bella looked across at Tom and I could almost see the gears working in her mind. Without saying another word she flounced away, heading directly for Tom.

"Poor Tom's going to disappoint yet another girl," Jack said. We went to the dance floor. Bella had gotten rid of Tom's partner and now was dancing with him and basically throwing herself at him. She kept touching his arm and his body, and leaning in close to whisper things in his ear. Tom was smiling but awkward, and I felt slightly sorry that I inflicted Bella on him. Jack and I danced for a while and then I saw Jonas and Peta. We broke off the dance floor and I walked off with Peta while Jack went to talk to his brother.

"Can you believe what everyone looks like?" Peta said to me.

"It's weird. It's like some people have just been inflated," I said.

I wasn't trying to be mean but hey, I'd had a few drinks.

It was about then that my cousins came over with Ollie and Will, Jack and Jonas walking behind them.

Molly and Luce had looked fine at home, little black dress, nice make up, but now they looked simply radiant. I couldn't tear my eyes away from them. Molly's eyes were like deep luminous pools and I just wanted to look at her all night long.

"Hey girls," Molly purred.

"What's happening?" Luce said from beside her, looking simply magnificent.

"Why are you two so beautiful?" I said, mesmerized. Then the answer hit me like a bolt of lightning. "Do you have your magic back? Is this a spell?" I said.

"A spell? What are you talking about? I always look like this," Molly said.

I pointed my finger at my cousins. "It's a potion isn't it? Where did you get it, because I want some for the next time I see Bella Bing," I said.

Molly and Luce shared a glance and then Luce nodded.

"Go and see Kira. She brewed it up for us," she said.

Before I could do that though, Bella joined our small circle. She started when she looked at Molly and how supernaturally beautiful she was.

"Hi Bella, you look tired. Have you been getting enough sleep?" Molly said with a warm smile and a sharp tone to her voice.

Bella shook off her amazement but instead of coming back with snark, she just sighed. She had a glass of wine in her hand and was fiddling with it.

"Can I ask you something important?" she said to Molly.

"Is it about how we are all engaged and have loving partners and you don't?" Molly said, wrapping her arm around Ollie.

Although Bella was a horror to go to school with and had been consistently mean to us, even I winced at the sharpness of Molly's response.

"We were friends… why did you abandon me?" Bella said in a small voice.

I could hear the band playing behind us, people talking, but it felt like it had all dropped away and the entire world had narrowed down to our little group. This wasn't Bella putting on a show or setting us up for something mean.

"What do you mean? Yeah, we were friends, but then we weren't, it happens," Molly said, stumbling a bit with her words.

"You had a family and I had *nothing*. You know that my father used to beat me. He didn't even *feed me* sometimes. I used to come out to your house as a sanctuary and you would share your food with me when I had none. We were best friends and then one day you said you wouldn't share your food with me because I was getting *fat*. You were the only good thing I had, and suddenly you weren't my friend anymore and I was alone," Bella said.

There was nothing but dead silence after Bella spoke. The pain from the past was real and immediate. My memories of that time back then were vague but it was true that Molly and Bella had been best friends for years, and Bella had been at our house many times. The two of them were inseparable. I guess if I had to admit it to myself I was vaguely aware of Bella's family troubles, too.

"I was interested in James Disher. You flirted with him, so he didn't like me anymore and I didn't want a friend who did that to me," Molly said. She crossed her arms and was looking upset.

"So you abandoned me and threw away our entire friendship over that? I was fourteen years old. My best friend ghosted me and I had no one and nowhere to go," Bella said.

"What you want? I was a teenager too. If you get excused for the things you did back then, then so do I," Molly said.

"You had everything I wanted. You had a loving mom and aunts and food, a safe place, and for a while, I had that too, then you took it away," Bella said.

Then she walked away, leaving all of us standing in silence.

Ollie carefully put his arm around Molly and she gave a sigh that was on the brink of tears.

"It wasn't the way she said it was... but I can see how was too. I feel bad I did that to her and I knew about her dad too. But I was fourteen. It's not an age where your empathy is at its peak," Molly said, as though she was trying to explain it to herself.

"Well she's still here, there's still time to make up for the past," I said. Our group broke up then, Molly and Ollie heading for the bar and the rest of us grabbing a drink too.

"Wow, that was painful," Jack said to me.

"You know, I saw some people tonight and those old tensions that I thought existed just vanished. Like, why was I ever afraid of them, or why did I ever care? Then there are other things from back then and they're still real. The pain is still raw and just waiting to be pulled out again," I said.

We had a bit more to drink and pulled ourselves back to the dance floor to shake off the dark mood. It wasn't long before Molly and Luce and their boyfriends were out with us, as well as Peta and Jonas. It also wasn't long before Bella was back out on the dance floor. She had done something to her top and pushed a lot more cleavage into view. She came up right beside me and tapped me on the shoulder.

"May have this dance with Jack?" she asked. There were people all around us and I felt like I was under observation.

"Sure, go ahead," I said in a chirpy voice and then walked off the dance floor looking for Kira.

"Salvador Dali," I whispered to Kira as I passed her. She broke away from the couple she was serving and followed me over to the table.

"What is it H-bomb? Do you need me to cast a spell on someone?" she asked.

"I need some of that potion you gave Molly and Luce," I said.

"Say no more," Kira said. She waved over her boyfriend Fox who delivered a glass of champagne and then went off to continue serving guests. Kira then retrieved a small bottle from her pocket and put a few drops of it into the champagne.

"Just drink it up and you'll be beautiful. It should last until about one in the morning. Good luck," Kira said and then zipped away to continue serving food. I was just reaching for my glass when Jack was at the side of the table, panting like he'd been running a marathon.

"That song was way too fast to dance to," he said, gulping in air. Before I could stop him he grabbed the glass of champagne and gulped it down in one giant mouthful.

I jumped to my feet in alarm.

"What is it?" Jack said, looking at me.

"Um... I'm not sure. Just sit here, don't do anything," I said. I looked around for Kira and saw her serving food to another table. I walked as close as I could. "Salvador Dali, Salvador Dali now," I called out. Kira came rushing over.

"What is it now? Is the potion not working?" she said.

"Jack drank it accidentally. Is anything going to happen?" I said.

Kira bit her fingernail.

"Men aren't meant to drink it. I... I don't know what's gonna happen. Maybe nothing," she said. We both looked over at Jack who was sitting at the table, watching us. He seemed unaffected so far.

"He looks okay," Kira said.

"Do you have an antidote or something?"

"It's a beauty potion. I didn't think I'd need an antidote," Kira said.

I rushed back to my table and looked Jack over again.

"Do you want to tell me what's going on?" he asked.

I explained that he had drunk a potion that was intended to make me beautiful, the same one that Molly and Luce had drunk, and that we didn't know what would happen.

"Well, I feel okay, maybe we should just keep having fun and if anything happens we can bolt out of here," Jack said.

Before I could I answer he grabbed me by the hand and we headed for the dance floor. We didn't get far though before we ran into Molly, Luce, Will and Ollie.

"Look at what Bella is doing now," Molly said, pointing towards the dance floor.

Bella was dancing with Chester, my boyfriend for four days all those years ago. He had a slightly bemused look on his face as Bella danced all over him.

"Well, at least it looks like she is feeling better," I said.

"I am going to apologize to her, I just need a little time," Molly said.

"Oh, hey, it's the Torrents…" a voice from behind us said. We turned around to see Richie Coldwell standing there in a disheveled suit. It was clear he had been drinking. Off in the background standing against the wall with her arms crossed was Natalia, glaring at everything.

"Are you here to destroy the school and then make a lowball offer on it?" Molly asked.

"Maybe you can call in a health violation on the canteen and try to have it shut down and then buy it six months later for a song," I added, unable to stop myself.

"What, are you gonna invite us up to your spa?" Luce said and then we all laughed at him.

Richie Coldwell went from smiling to sad in an instant.

"Did you ever think that when I was asking you to come to my house that was maybe just because I wanted friends and didn't have any?" he mumbled before walking away.

Oh no.

"Did I hurt his feelings? Should I go after him?" Luce asked, worried.

"I think it's going to be fine," I said, pointing over near the bar. Richie had joined a group of men doing shots and cheering after each one.

"Somehow I think with years of therapy he's going to come to forgive you," Molly said.

"I need to dance, now," I said and grabbed Jack. We didn't

make it two steps before suddenly there she was in front of me. Abby Crookshank.

"Harlow, I need to talk to you," she said. Oh boy, it was clear that she'd been drinking too.

"Hi Abby," I said.

"I was such a bitc–" she burped and recovered. "I was so mean to you guys, I'm sorry," she said.

"It's okay," I said automatically. It was true that Abby had been horrible but honestly she'd been a minor player in an entire cast of bullies. Because I was a Slip Witch I was often out of school due to magical mishaps which sort of made me an outsider. If I didn't have my cousins for support I don't know what I would have done. Although Abby had been a minor bully she did stab me with a pencil once.

"It's not okay, I feel really bad about it. I shouldn't have done it to you. Please forgive me," she said.

She looked like she was about to cry. What was my responsibility here? Did I have to make people I'd likely never see again feel better? I didn't want to spend the rest my night playing confession and absolution with drunk people.

"I forgive you, it's okay, really," I said, desperate to get away. Thankfully, Jack took charge, grabbed me by the arm and took me away. I saw a man I assumed to be Abby's husband take hold of her and lead her away also.

Jack and I hit the dance floor and soon we pushed that dark mood away. The night had been fun, but punctuated with moments of sadness. We soon left the dance floor and I bumped into a few other people and caught up with them, knowing that I'd likely never see some of them ever again. I met people who I couldn't remember whatsoever, and others who told me of memories of us together. It was as though they were holding *my* memories in *their* heads because once they told me I could recollect it.

The night was wearing on, the band had stopped and now

just random songs were playing through the sound system. The teenage waiters had stopped circulating with food, and as people had left the crowd had gathered over near the bar in a small area. I saw that Tom and his husband Edward had left, as well as many others, including Jonas and Peta. Richie was still with the group of men drinking heavily and laughing raucously. I couldn't see Bella Bing anywhere and now that I thought about it I didn't see Chester either. Had they left together?

"Hieronymus Bosch!" I heard Molly call out.

"Salvador Dali!" I heard Luce say. I turned around to see them standing by Jack.

"Oh my Goddess," I whispered to myself.

He suddenly had a full beard. It was black and thick and he looked like a lumberjack. Even in the second I stood there, I could see it growing. It must be Kira's potion.

"Um… Francisco Guyer! Pablo Picasso! Renee Magritte!" I called out, trying to alert Will and Ollie as well as Kira. Luce, Molly and I grabbed Jack and hustled him out of there so fast his feet barely touched the ground. We rushed out the side door and away from the hall, heading for the darkness. Even in the few steps we'd taken Jack's beard had grown longer and I saw his eyebrows were sprouting too. Will and Ollie came bursting out of the hall from behind us with Kira following close behind them.

We rushed into the dark heading as far away from people as we could and finally stopped around the side of an old classroom. The moon was still full and floating above. Jack's beard was now down to his waist and his eyebrows were long and hanging down over his face.

"We need to get some scissors," Jack said, pushing his eyebrows back.

"Kira do you know how to stop this?" Molly asked.

The teenager was panicking. "I don't know how to make

an antidote to this. I didn't think I would need one, boys aren't meant to drink it," she wailed.

"It's okay, Kira, it's just some hair and it looks like it's slowing down already," I said.

"I'm going to get some scissors, come on Will," Luce said and vanished off into the darkness with Will behind her. Jack's beard kept growing and was now dangling down past his waist and his eyebrows were simply ridiculous, two long black waterfalls that went down his face. But whatever effect the potion was having was wearing off. Soon his beard stopped growing and his eyebrows too.

"This is the best school reunion I've ever been to," Jack said, trying to make a joke. I laughed, but I was also extremely worried that someone would see us. None of us had any magic to cover this up and I don't know if Kira could cast a concealment spell to hide Jack away, especially if a lot of people saw us.

Luce soon returned with a pair of scissors.

"And now we've broken into a school to steal scissors," Will said. I grabbed the scissors and in the light of a few phones cut Jack's beard off and trimmed his eyebrows back. It wasn't a perfect job and he still looked quite scruffy, but it was better than what he looked like before. We stuffed the long beard and eyebrows into a trashcan and then Luce grabbed the scissors and disappeared off into the darkness with Will again. It wasn't long before she was back. having returned the scissors and then all of us could relax.

"That was a crazy night," Will commented.

"Abby Crookshank apologized to me so that's something," I said.

We went wandering away from the building, heading directly towards the trees where Jack and I'd carved our initials earlier. We ended up sitting in front of it and talking. We were also sobering up from the endless bottomless glasses of white wine. As we were sitting there a few clouds scudded across the moon, casting us into shadow.

"I really am going to find Bella and apologize," Molly said again.

"Well I feel better that Abby apologized to me," I said. I'd surprised even myself by saying that, but it was true. There were old wounds left from the past, and even though Abby had been drunk her apology helped soothe some of them.

We sat around in the warm dark talking until we judged that we'd all sobered up enough to drive home. It was almost two by that point. As we were making our way back towards the hall and our cars we heard a sudden rustling from some bushes over in the dark.

Although all three of us witches were very relaxed and somewhat tired, we grabbed our boyfriends and pulled them into the darkness to hide away. I think we were all on high alert in case anything else magical might happen. It was then we saw Bella emerge from the bushes, fixing up her clothing and behind her, Chester. Bella gave him a passionate kiss and wrapped her arms around him, and then they walked away together.

"Oh, this is too perfect, Molly whispered, getting ready to bust them. I put my hand on her arm.

"No, let her have this," I said.

"Fine," Molly said. Once Bella and Chester were gone we headed back to the cars. The hall was now closed and dark and the night was silent. It was then that the piercing sound of a fire siren broke the night.

The three of us may have been without magic but we weren't without intuition.

"What is that?" I called out. I could see a red glow in the dark that looked like it was in the direction of Jack's house that he was renovating.

"Let's go!" Molly called out. We pulled our respective

boyfriends into our cars and took off through the night. I was beside Jack as he drove, a ball of tension in my stomach. All I could imagine was his beautiful renovated house burning to the ground. Perhaps revenge from Richie Coldwell for treating him badly tonight. As we got closer, hearing more sirens in the night, I realized it wasn't Jack's house but a few streets away. When we turned the corner that ball of tension in my stomach turned to ice and I felt sick. I knew whose house was on fire before I even saw it.

We parked and I stumbled out of Jack's truck, barely able to hold myself up straight. All the strength had gone out of my legs. It was Carter's house, and it was fully ablaze. The firefighters were trying to put it out and there were gathered police cars. Out on the street, Constance Osterman was standing in a white nightgown that was stained with ash. She was sobbing and fighting with one of the police officers who was trying to hold her back. I stumbled closer, seeing some of the neighbors had come out of their homes before I tripped and fell. Jack was somewhere beside me helping me stand up and then I was sobbing, an intense pain in my heart. I saw Sheriff Hardy. He was directing his men to keep onlookers back. As he came close to us, I couldn't help but call out.

"Where's Carter?" I said. Sheriff Hardy cast a look back towards the house and towards Constance to make sure she was out of earshot.

"We think he's still inside," he said, his voice grim, before he walked away. The roof of the house collapsed, sending glowing red sparks pluming up into the night sky.

CHAPTER FIFTEEN

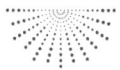

I stared at the article, my mind blank. All the facts were there. It was complete. Carter's house burning down, Constance asleep in the front room and escaping. Her advising that Carter had been working in a back room as far as she'd been aware. The attendance of the fire brigade and the police, how there were no witnesses, how the roof had collapsed. I'd even thrown in the journalistic cliché of "There are grave concerns for Carter's safety". The translation for that was that we suspected he was dead but we hadn't yet found the body.

At the thought of it, that Carter was truly gone, tears threatened to well again and I squinted to them push away. I just couldn't think about it or I'd descend into sobbing. As it was I'd spent a lot of the night doing that in between broken bouts of sleep.

I opened my eyes and looked over my article again. Carter's four boxes of files were still sitting on the sofa behind me. I should be publishing this article on the *Harlot Bay Times* website. I should hand over the files to Sheriff Hardy or hide them at home, work out a way to destroy

Coldwell with them. But I was numb, tired and scared. Sheriff Hardy and his men were looking for the two goons, Clifford and Lazarus, in our opinion the prime suspects for the arson. I hadn't yet told Sheriff Hardy that it was me, Molly and Luce who had broken into Sylvester Coldwell's office and stolen his files (although he probably knew it was us). But I planned to call him out to the mansion later today and hand the files over. There was solid proof there that Sylvester Coldwell had files on our family and on Carter, and also the two suspected arsonists were in there as well. I don't know how Sheriff Hardy would be able to use the files, considering we had stolen them but I didn't really know what else to do at this point.

I eventually published the article on to the *Harlot Bay Times* website. Now that Carter was gone I was the sole employee. I tried to pull my mind away from these dark thoughts, but it was difficult. Where I was sitting now in the comfortable numbness was a better place. In one direction was an endless well of tears and sadness. In the other, dark fury so complete that it terrified me. I felt the desire to give into it. That I'd get my magic back and hunt down those two men... destroy them utterly. Despite my desire to stay in this numb place I felt my thoughts grow darker. It seemed evident that if we didn't stop who was behind the attacks that it could just get worse. Someone had already thrown a Molotov through the window of the *Chili Challenge* when Aunt Cass was there. What would be next? The Torrent Mansion burning to the ground? Me, Molly or Luce being shot? To pull myself out of that darkness I went over to the boxes of files and pulled out a random bunch before sitting back at my desk. I was flicking through them when there was a hesitant tap on the door.

"Come in," I said automatically.

It was Hattie Stern but not as she normally appeared.

Most of the time Hattie appeared to be clad in invisible armor. She always seemed to be looking down at you and had a judgmental tone in her voice.

I knew in my heart that part of it was façade, after all, she had helped train me a long time ago and I'd caught glimpses of her has a warm grandmother. But those moments were few and far between. She always reverted to her stone cold demeanor. But not now. She seemed nervous, fretting. She had a piece of fabric in her hands that she was pulling at.

"Harlow... there's... something is wrong," Hattie said. She was hovering in the doorway as though unsure about whether she should enter.

"There's a lot wrong. A house has burnt down and Carter's dead. Someone threw a Molotov at Aunt Cass's business and sabotaged ours. There are bad people in town doing bad things and they aren't going to stop until someone stops them. Is that what you're talking about?" I asked. I wasn't mean, but I was numb and exhausted.

"It's something else, Harlow. Something is very, very wrong. I don't remember. I feel like I know something and that's gone. Do you know what it is?" she asked me.

I heard a tiny voice whisper *there is a spell on you* but I dismissed it. Whatever Hattie was talking about I didn't need any of it all. I had enough on my plate by a mile and if she didn't have anything clear to say then I didn't want to hear it.

"I don't know what you're talking about Hattie, I need to go back to work," I said, a chill tone entering my voice.

Hattie looked at me, worried. She was biting her lip and looked on the verge of panic. "I think someone is missing, someone is gone," she muttered before turning away and hurrying down the stairs.

I put her out of my mind , standing up to close the door and then returning to the files that Carter had left me. I was still disconnected from the magic thanks to Aunt Cass and her slip, and honestly it made me feel I didn't want to know anything about magical things. It had occurred to me that this is what I'd wanted for many years, to not be a slip witch at all, to be normal, but now it was here it felt lonely. The warm flow of magic was always comforting, to feel it close at hand. But now it was gone and yet we couldn't help but find ourselves entangled in situations where magic could be very useful.

Another hour passed, me reading files, drifting along in the numb, when there was another tap on the door.

"Come in," I sighed.

It was Sylvester Coldwell. He stepped inside and closed the door behind him. I jumped up from my chair and took two steps back, putting the desk between us. It wasn't the best of moves. The only place I had to go now was out the front window and I didn't particularly feel like taking that risk.

"I'm not going to hurt you," Sylvester said.

He looked tired, unshaven. He was wearing a suit but there was a stain on the shirt. He seemed sober but it appeared it was a rare moment between bouts of drinking.

"Get out of here before I call the police," I warned. Coldwell took a step towards me, but then stopped when I jumped further back, heading to the window.

"I didn't kill him, Harlow, I promise," he said.

I could feel the darkness roaring in my mind, the anger coming cold and sharp like a knife.

"But you're going to be the prime suspect Sylvester. You had run-ins with Carter before, he was reporting on your family, and you've threatened him. You have a long history of being involved with arsonists," I said, spitting venom.

Coldwell shook his head, his eyes pleading with me. "I'm just trying to run my business. I had nothing to do with his death. None of this is good for me. I don't make any money if a journalist who's been writing about me dies. Don't you understand that? The mall project is worth millions. If I'm under investigation for murder how do you think that's going to go? How could I possibly benefit from taking out some small-time reporter? Most of the people who read his paper are in their eighties," Coldwell said.

"Sunny Days Manor—were you trying to run that into the ground so you could buy it? Didn't some men turn up with a plan to burn it down so then you could buy?" I said.

It seemed like it had been a lifetime ago, but we had uncovered a plot, it seemed, to ruin the Sunny Days Manor so Coldwell could buy it cheaply. He'd been running the place and standards had gone downhill, the residents being served moldy food, needed renovation not being done. Thanks to my intervention Coldwell had been removed by the actual owners of the nursing home.

Coldwell looked at me and I could see he was trying to keep himself calm, but I just didn't care.

"All that stuff isn't important now. Don't you understand? I think someone killed Carter so I could be blamed," he said.

"And I hope you are. I hope to see you go to prison for the rest of your disgusting life," I said.

"You know, I didn't have anything to do with that pathetic coffee shop being sabotaged nor that rundown wreck of the mansion you live in. But I absolutely wish I had. I wish I'd thrown the Molotov cocktail through that ridiculous *Chili Challenge* warehouse window. But it wasn't me. It was someone else and aren't you meant to be a journalist? Aren't you meant to be seeking the truth?"

He was angry, raising his voice, waving his arms around. But it meant nothing to me. As far as I was concerned, he was a murderer, just as equally to blame as those men who had burnt Carter's house down. He had tried to destroy my cousins' business, had attacked Aunt Cass's, and shut down the Moms' bed and breakfast.

"Please just go away and *die*," I said.

"I knew this would be a waste of time," Coldwell muttered. He left my office, slamming the door behind him.

There was a flimsy lock on the door, but I used it anyway. I didn't want to see anyone else appear. What was clear to me now was that I had to get the files out of my office. For all I knew they were the final copy now that Carter's house was gone. And Coldwell had been standing right next to them. I couldn't know what he had seen. Once I calmed down enough, I carried the boxes one by one down to my car which was parked down on the street and loaded the trunk. I was just leaving town when my phone chimed a message. It was from Mom.

Emergency family meeting right now!

I sighed as I looked up the hill towards our mansion.

What now?

CHAPTER SIXTEEN

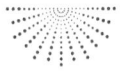

Aunt Cass was standing out the front of the Torrent Mansion and she was drinking a beer.

"Okaay…" I said to myself as I parked and got out of the car. I walked over, my feet crunching on the gravel.

"Little early isn't it?" I asked.

"Five o'clock somewhere plus it's a celebration beer. Look at this," Aunt Cass said and she let a golden spark go from the tip of her finger.

"Your magic is back?" I asked amazed.

"Not quite, but it's getting there. It won't be long now," she said.

"Has this emergency family meeting started yet or do we have time?" I asked, a sudden idea popping into my mind.

Aunt Cass took a swig of her beer. "Your cousins aren't even here yet so I think we have time, " she said.

"I need you to cast a finding spell to locate the man who burnt down Carter's house," I said.

"Let's roll," Aunt Cass said.

We rushed down to my end of the mansion and went up into the roof space to retrieve the files that we'd stolen from

Sylvester Coldwell's office. Inside them were the two photographs of Clifford and Lazarus.

Finding spells are quite simple. Grab the magic, focus on what you want, usually by looking at a photograph of holding an object that they may have owned, and then you whisper "Find". A ball of light leads the way.

Aunt Cass picked up Clifford's photo, let out a breath and whispered "Find". A minuscule dot of light drifted up from her finger and started heading towards the door before winking out of existence. Aunt Cass sat down at the kitchen table and yawned.

"No, that's too much right now, we're going to have to wait a few days," she said.

"But we need to find those guys before they hurt anyone else. We should ask Kira!" I said. I couldn't believe I hadn't thought of it earlier: use a finding spell, locate them, call Sheriff Hardy, get them arrested.

"No, you can't. I promised Hattie," Aunt Cass said. I sighed.

"What about her friend Sophira? She's a slip witch too. She could do it," I said.

Aunt Cass shook her head again. "Harlow, it needs to be one of us. We can't pull other witches into this, it's just too dangerous," she said.

"But Carter is dead. It's just a finding spell. Isn't that important?" I asked.

Aunt Cass looked at me and then nodded. "It is important, but it is up to us. It's far too dangerous to get anyone else involved. We don't want them to become pieces on the chessboard," she said.

I saw my amazing plan come crashing to the ground. But I guess not all hope was lost. If Aunt Cass had her magic back already then who knows, even by tonight or tomorrow she would be able to cast a finding spell and surely it wouldn't be long before me or my cousins or the Moms had our magic back too.

"Okay, fine. We'll just wait a little longer until we have our magic back and do it ourselves," I said.

My phone chimed a message from Mom telling me to come back for the emergency family meeting. Me and Aunt Cass walked back, Aunt Cass finishing off the rest of her beer and then tossing the empty bottle into some bushes so the Moms wouldn't see it. As we walked in I heard her burp quietly into her hand. The Moms and my cousins were gathered in the lounge and up on the board was the map that we'd found under the mansion again.

"Finally you're here, Harlow. Take a seat," Mom said.

"They only just got here, so don't make out like I'm super late," I said, pointing to Molly and Luce and gambling on the chance they'd actually just got there.

"Hey, don't pull us into it just because you're late," Molly said, throwing me under the bus.

I grumbled to myself as I took a seat.

Mom took the floor. "We have alarms being installed everywhere: at *Traveler*, at Big Pie, at the rebuilt bakery site, at *The Cozy Cat*, down at the *Chili Challenge*. Everywhere. It might even be an idea to get your boyfriends to put them in their homes," Mom said.

"We already know this. Is this why you called us in?" I grumbled, still a little annoyed at being told off for being late.

"Ollie discovered something actually dear, and it's about something far more important than what has been happening in Harlot Bay," Mom said sweetly, but with an undercurrent of sarcasm.

She went to the side of the room and picked up a small lamp and carried it over near the map. She turned it on and then lifted the bottom of the map up to hold the light behind it. As she did, writing appeared on the map and also the drawing of a line heading out from Harlot Bay across the water and onto Truer Island.

"This is a set of instructions on how to reach the mansion out on Truer Island. Ollie discovered it and he has tied dates in that journal to other papers he's found. Juliet Stern and Marguerite Torrent were hunters tracking down bad witches and monsters. After their encounter with the Shadow Witch they doubled their efforts until their husbands disappeared. Juliet had another daughter. A few years after that, both Juliet and Marguerite vanished themselves, leaving their daughters behind. We believe that for some reason Marguerite cursed her own daughter before leaving, and that curse has carried on down to us," Mom said.

"A curse? But what kind of curse?" Luce asked biting her nails.

"Well what has been happening to us, darling?" Aunt Freya said. "The attacks on the mansion and *Traveler* and *Chili Challenge*. Murders and sabotage. How many times have we been pulled into things in Harlot Bay? No matter how much we try to stay out of it we get tangled up in murder, arson and death. What else could it be but a curse?"

"Why would our own ancestor do that to us?" Molly asked.

"When slip witches go bad, they don't care about anyone," Aunt Cass said, her voice dark.

I glanced across at her. She looked troubled. I could feel it too. We were the only two slip witches in the room and it wasn't good knowing that you had the possibility of slipping into the darkness, turning evil and then hurting people you formally loved.

"We believe that you three girls were able to find the mansion because you followed the instructions on the map that you found. But it was one use only. And as soon as you left you couldn't find it again. But now we've found another set of instructions. Whatever is out there, maybe it's Marguerite or something else, we can go out there and confront it. If it *is* her we can destroy her and end the curse on us forever," Mom said.

The room was dead silent which, if you know the Torrent witches is extremely unusual. I found myself shaking my head. What other problems do we need to be loaded down on top of us? We were under direct threat from two crazed arsonists who had already taken a life and now we had to deal with this as well? Sure, we had found a room full of weapons, but the Moms were kitchen witches, Aunt Cass was in her eighties, my cousins ran a café, and I was writing a book whilst working as a waitress and a sometime journalist. I had ridden along inside my ancestor's mind as she and Juliet were tracking down the Shadow Witch. She was trained, experienced. If we went out there, we would be lambs to the slaughter.

"But we don't have any magic," Aunt Ro said, looking at Mom.

"We have weapons though, and Aunt Cass has some. I think we need to go as soon as possible before the curse gets worse," Mom said.

The room erupted into a cacophony of argument. Mom wanted to go, the sooner the better. Aunt Freya was on her side. Me, Molly and Luce wanted to wait until our magic returned at the very least. I think secretly we wished we didn't have to go at all. But there had been something in what Mom had said to us. When we looked back over our lives, we could see it punctuated by a series of terrible events. I returned to Harlot Bay after the apartment block I'd been living in had burnt to the ground. Molly and Luce had had their coffee machine stolen, their business almost destroyed. I'd been swept up in more mysterious events than I could count.

The argument seemed it would never end until Aunt Cass stood up and flicked her hand, shooting a few golden sparks out in front of us that crackled to the floor like tiny fireworks.

"As ranking witch here I say we go when our magic returns and not a moment sooner. And I don't want to hear any more about it," Aunt Cass said.

"You're not ranking witch. That's not even a thing," Mom protested.

"I think Aunt Cass is right, we definitely need magic if we are gonna do this," Luce said.

Mom turned to her. "You do realize then if she's ranking witch, that means we outrank you and you're at the bottom of the totem pole."

"That's okay. I'm okay with that," Luce said hurriedly.

The argument petered out after that. Aunt Cass glared everybody down and so we all agreed we would go out to the mansion once our magic returned. We would see if Marguerite Torrent, our ancestor, was out there and if she was we would destroy her and end the curse that was on our family. It wasn't long after that I was walking with my cousins back to our end of the mansion.

"I am so glad Ollie didn't see that," Molly said in a quiet voice.

"Yeah, this is way too much witchiness even for me," Luce said. We went inside our end of the mansion to find Adams and Hugo sitting on the sofa watching television together, a bowl of popcorn between them. The day felt laden down with stress and anxiety and I had no idea what I would tell Jack about what we had just decided. I had long ago decided to tell him the truth about things but still, I didn't always tell him *all* the truth. What would I say to him now? "Oh, by the way Jack our entire family is under a curse that pulls us into terrible events and once our magic's back we're all going to go out to Truer Island to see if we can destroy a witch who might be our great great great grandmother. Be home for dinner!"

I shook my head to myself as I slumped down on the sofa beside Adams. I reached over to take a handful of buttery popcorn.

"So what are we watching guys?" I asked as I focused on the television.

"It's a documentary about how to make wine," Adams said.

I settled in next to my cat to watch, and Molly and Luce did the same. There was an unspoken agreement between us. It was far better to sit and watch television than accept the reality of our lives. Soon we would have to face the darkness that felt ready to engulf us.

CHAPTER SEVENTEEN

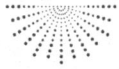

*D*ays slipped by in rapid succession. Firefighters were still digging through the ruins of Carter's house but it was slow going. Like most properties in Harlot Bay it had an attic, a basement, and another entire floor beneath it. This had all burnt down and collapsed in on itself. It was possibly going to take months to dig it all out. Everything had been at high tension but then nothing had happened and as the days went by the recent past took on an unearthly feel as though it couldn't possibly have been real. I found myself at Jack's most nights and during the days I was often at home reading the files on Coldwell. I was still publishing on the *Harlot Bay Times* website but it was the general news around town and it was sparse at that. Because it was only me, there was no way I could keep up.

I heard that Carter's elderly parents were in town but I hadn't seen them yet. The family was getting ready to have a funeral with an empty casket.

I was sitting there in front of my computer again reading over some of the articles that Carter had published before the fire, when Sylvester Coldwell came through the door. And I mean *through* the door.

"Oh Goddess, no," I whispered.

He was a ghost.

Which meant he was dead.

"You *can* see me," Coldwell said triumphantly.

I stood up from my desk but didn't back away like last time. Ghosts had no power over the living. All it would take to get rid of Coldwell was to poke him with my finger and he'd go bouncing away like a rubber ball. I looked him up and down. He was wearing his suit and he looked immaculate, not a hair out of place. The fact I could see him was incredible. No one's magic had returned and Aunt Cass was still stuck at her low level, only being able to fling the occasional spark from the end of her finger. Did this mean my magic was coming back? I tried to summon a light but failed.

"I know you can see me. Someone murdered me, Harlow," Coldwell said, his voice booming.

I nodded, trying to gather my thoughts. The last few days of nothing had been greatly needed, a reprieve from dark times but suddenly I was plunged back into it. I also couldn't help but remember what I'd said to Coldwell when he had last been in my office.

Please just go die.

"Who murdered you?" I asked.

Coldwell drifted over to the sofa and sat down on it. He was so insubstantial that he didn't even disturb the dust. "I think it was..." He frowned, unable to remember.

"It's okay. Do you know where your body is?" I asked.

Coldwell shook his head. "Why can't I remember?" he asked.

"It's a common ghost problem. Ghosts don't want to confront the fact they're dead and gone," I said. I know it may have sounded like I was harsh and abrupt, but the fastest way to get a ghost to move on was to make them realize that they had no connection to the world anymore. Most ghosts barely made it through their first day, given they couldn't touch anything or talk to anyone. I also had a fear that Coldwell could possibly turn bad. I'd seen it before, and if anyone was going to turn into some kind of screaming poltergeist I suspected it would be him.

"Please, my children, Ritchie and Natalia, you have to help protect them. They're going to be next," Coldwell said.

"How do you know that?" I asked. I pulled my phone out of my pocket and rang the Sheriff's office.

"I don't know, but they are," Coldwell said, growing agitated. I saw the slight outline around him begin to darken.

I got the receptionist, Mary who put me straight through to Sheriff Hardy. "I need you at my office right now Sheriff it's vitally important. I need to see you immediately," I said.

"Are you in any danger? Say to me 'Yes, bring coffee' if there is danger," Sheriff said.

"I'm not in any danger, but I need to see you straight away, please come here," I said. Sheriff Hardy said he'd see me in a few minutes and then hung up the phone.

"Can you help me?" Coldwell asked. I glanced over at him. I didn't like the way his aura kept getting darker.

"I will help you, and I'll help your children, I promise, you just need to think of happier things, stay positive," I said.

I had no idea whether that was the right thing to say, but thankfully his aura began to lighten. It wasn't long before Sheriff Hardy rapped on the door and came in without waiting for me to answer. He'd run up the stairs, and his face was turning red.

"What is it, Harlow?" the Sheriff puffed, looking about the room for any unknown assailant.

I moved past him and closed the door so no one could hear us.

LOST WITCH

"Sylvester Coldwell is dead. He is a ghost, and he's sitting right there on the sofa," I said.

Sheriff Hardy looked at the sofa, but obviously couldn't see anything. I saw him gather his thoughts, his professionalism as a police officer coming into play. He pulled a notepad out of his pocket and a pen.

"Do you mind if I sit at your desk and you can ask him questions?" Sheriff Hardy asked.

I waved my hand to my desk and Sheriff Hardy took a seat.

"Does he know where his body is?" Sheriff Hardy asked.

I took a deep breath and started what was sure to be a very long and frustrating interview.

CHAPTER EIGHTEEN

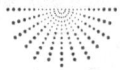

They found Sylvester's body early the next morning. He'd been shot and dumped off the end of the pier. Sheriff Hardy had rung me to give me the news. I drove myself back into town to my office where I found Coldwell waiting for me. Despite my strong desire to stay as far away as I could from misery and death, I went with him to the pier in the hope that he would remember what had happened to him and possibly identify the murderers or, better than that, move on.

I was standing there in the cold morning with Sylvester Coldwell floating beside me looking at the crime scene. He didn't remember a thing. He had no recollection of ever coming here, no memory of what he'd been doing before he'd been killed. Like many other ghosts his memory was riddled with holes. He couldn't even remember coming up to my office when he had claimed that he had nothing to do with Carter's house burning down.

I'd told him I would help keep Richie and Natalia safe but that had mostly been an act of desperation at seeing his aura darken. After the family and our respective boyfriends had discovered what had happened with Coldwell, there had been a lot of serious conversation about all of us simply leaving Harlot Bay. Maybe we would return to discover Torrent Mansion burnt down and *Traveler* and the *Chili Challenge*, but who cares about that? They were just buildings.

I was standing staring at the scene with Coldwell drifting beside me when the first national news van pulled up and I groaned.

The fire that had killed a small town journalist hadn't been enough to attract attention but the death of a major real estate developer? That was like rotting meat to these vultures.

I watched as a reporter jumped out of the van with her microphone, the camera crew following close behind her. She stood with her back to the crime scene, and although I couldn't hear her speaking I could easily imagine what she was saying. They always recited the same trite clichés.

"The small town of Harlot Bay is once again the scene of tragedy…" I murmured to myself.

"I need to go back to my office now, can you please look around town for a chubby man with spiky blond hair?" I asked Coldwell.

I had my phone up against my ear so it didn't look like I was talking to nothing.

"I will," Coldwell said earnestly before drifting away.

I know it was pointless giving him that task. Every time I saw him he'd forgotten that I had told him to do it, and he would once again ask me about protecting Richie and Natalia.

I went back to my car and then drove over to my office, parking outside it. I walked up the stairs, hearing the television playing at low volume. I expected to find John Smith in there but the office was empty, the TV on by itself. I flicked it off and sat down on the sofa, raising a small cloud of dust.

Maybe Jack was right, we should just leave. The police would eventually do their job and hopefully find the murderers.

I spent the first part of the morning doing more research on Sylvester Coldwell's dealings. Yes, he was deceased but that didn't mean that any crimes he'd committed were finished. It was around ten when I received a new email message. It was from someone calling themselves *The Truth*.

There was nothing in the message except for a video. When I opened it, I saw it was of August Coldwell. The video was grainy as though it was taken from a great distance. August was meeting with a man who was in shadow. I saw the man pass him something and then walk away. For a moment, the man passed into a beam of light and I saw a flash of blond hair before the video clip ended.

I saved the video clip to my computer and then sent another copy to my private email account so I could have a backup.

The video quality was terrible, but was that proof that August Coldwell was meeting the thug Clifford? It seemed too coincidental that he'd be meeting with a blond-haired man. I composed a message.

Dear Truth, where did you get this? Where was it filmed? Please send me any information you have on August Coldwell immediately.

I sent the message and then sat there at my desk, my heart pounding. I had a brief moment of indecision about whether I should send it to Sheriff Hardy too given that I didn't want to get tangled up with the police, but eventually I decided I would send it to him. Anything that could be used to bring the men who had murdered Carter and now Coldwell to justice. I emailed the video to Sheriff Hardy at the police station and then I spent the rest of the morning looking into August Coldwell.

It was only when my phone chimed a message that I remembered I had arranged to have lunch with Peta and Jonas. I hadn't gotten far with August Coldwell so it wasn't too much of a big deal to be pulled away from my work. As I rushed downstairs I realized I hadn't heard Jonas come in this morning. I knocked on his door, but it was locked. Maybe he hadn't come in at all today. I drove over to The Curry Cauldron to find Jonas and Peta waiting for me.

"Let's eat, I'm starving," Peta said.

Jonas just grunted at me and then yawned. We went inside the darkened restaurant and sat down and started looking through our menus. I knew why Peta had called this lunch for me—to try to stop me falling into depression, which was a real risk at the moment. She was chatting away about anything and everything: The school reunion; her business *The Cozy Cat*; the Governor's mansion renovations. Anything to distract me. Soon our food was served and we began eating, although Jonas soon put down his fork and took a sip of water to wash the flavor of the food from his mouth.

"Is there something wrong?" I asked.

Jonas shook his head and then rubbed his eyes again. "I think I must be coming down with something. I've been feeling groggy and sick all day," he said.

"It wasn't too much wine last night?" I asked, trying to keep things light.

"No, I didn't have anything to drink. It was so weird too. I was so tired that I went to sleep on the sofa which I never do. I woke up there this morning, feeling terrible," he said.

Peta reached across and rubbed the back of his neck.

"Maybe we should get home after this, then," she said gently.

We finished up our lunch, part of me thinking that I hoped Jonas didn't have anything, and if he did that it wasn't contagious. I really didn't need a virus on top of everything else. After that I went back to my office to spend the rest of the afternoon in what was seeming to be a pointless task of looking into August Coldwell. It was around five when Jack rang. Since we'd been spending so much time together he almost always called late in the afternoon, often to ask me what I wanted to eat for dinner.

"I vote pizza," I said as soon as I answered the phone.

"Harlow, I need to…" Jack said, his voice strained.

I felt a cold shock wash over me.

"What's the matter?" I asked.

"It's Jonas. He's been arrested. They found a gun in his house and I think it was the one used to kill Sylvester Coldwell," Jack said.

CHAPTER NINETEEN

"Dry cat biscuits and hose water. Bon appétit," I said.

Adams looked at his breakfast in disgust. "I don't want to drink hose water," he yowled.

"Well maybe you and your mouse friend shouldn't have eaten all of our food then," I said.

Adams pushed some of the cat biscuits out of his bowl and onto the floor before sniffing at them.

"What are these? They don't smell good," he complained.

There are actually Adams's standard cat biscuits, except I'd slipped some of them into a plain white box that I had found. I picked it up from the counter and examined it.

"Not quite sure really. I think it was ex-military stock from Russia. They're plain flavored though," I said, making up a lie on the spot.

"Plain flavored? That's not a flavor!"

"Well, that's the way it is. Next time don't eat all our food," I said. It wasn't hose water either but Adams didn't know that.

The little cat started poking mournfully at the biscuits.

"Can I use some of my pocket money to buy different food?" he asked.

"You don't get pocket money," I reminded him.

"Can I start getting pocket money? I can do all sorts of useful things. Look, I can clean," he said trying to scrabble the cat biscuits that he had knocked out back into the bowl.

"No pocket money. Dry cat biscuits and hose water," I said and crossed my arms. I left Adams by his breakfast, staring at it glumly, and continued getting ready for the day. Three days had passed since Jonas had been arrested and it felt like the world had broken. Then it had turned out that it wasn't, and life had carried on. There were still meals to be eaten, we needed to sleep, and we had businesses to be run. Jack had gone from fear to anger to a type of cold competence over a matter of hours. He had now shut down all work at the Governor's mansion and had gone back to cop mode. The last time I'd spoken to him he'd told me he was almost ready to begin surveillance on August Coldwell, whom he blamed for framing his brother.

I was confident that something would come up, that Jonas would be cleared, but the deck was certainly stacked against him. The police had confirmed that the gun they'd found in Jonas's house was the same one that was used to kill Sylvester Coldwell. Jonas's fingerprints were all over it. It was only a day after Jonas had been arrested that Peta realized it was possible he may have been drugged so someone could break into his house to plant the gun. The police eventually had a doctor come in to take a blood sample from Jonas, but who knows if it would show up anything so many hours after the fact.

As for the rest of us, we were trying to continue on in our lives, albeit at a higher state of tension. The Moms were running the bakery. There were still no guests at the bed and breakfast. My cousins had *Traveler* open and were getting about two customers a day, and Peta had reopened *The Cozy Cat*, although it was still suffering from being associated with *Traveler* during its time of being shut down by the Health Department.

I had been spending my days trying to support Jack and working through Carter's files on Coldwell. Occasionally I would see Sylvester who would again demand that I protect Richie and Natalia, and have nothing useful to say on any other topic.

I'd just finished brushing my teeth and went down to the lounge room when Aunt Cass came racing in through the front door, grinning.

"Excellent you're here. Come with me," she said grabbing me by the hand.

"What is it?" I asked as she pulled me out the front door.

"Come on, keep up," Aunt Cass said, letting go of my hand and racing ahead, heading back to the main part of the mansion.

"Just tell me, is this something bad?" I called out. My Goddess she was fast.

"No, it's good!" Aunt Cass called out. We entered the mansion, and I followed her in through the kitchen and down the stairs. Someone had taken the sheet off Grandma April who was standing in the corner in the same pose she always was: hands out in front of her like she was holding an invisible ball, a slight smile on her face.

"Hey sis," Aunt Cass said as she passed, heading for the basement door.

"Hey Grandma," I said. Aunt Cass grabbed some flashlights and passed me one. I followed her into the warm dark under the mansion, headed down a few corridors and then suddenly there we were, at the door to Aunt Cass's lair. I'd only been in there once before, a very long time ago when she'd taken Kira and me there so we could help her set up beacons around the town in our efforts to track down what we thought was a monster. Since then I'd made other attempts to find her lair, given she had an entire wall that looked like something out of a serial killer's fantasy covered in articles and maps and bits of string, sticky notes, and pins. Aunt Cass carefully protected her lair and refused to let anyone else into it.

"Come on in," Aunt Cass said, opening the door and pulling me inside.

" I'm allowed to see your crazy lair," I said, unable to stop myself taking a little jab.

"Yes, yes, don't worry about that. Have a look at the wall," Aunt Cass said.

I turned my flashlight off and looked up at Aunt Cass's wall of crazy. I used to have a wall of crazy myself in one of the cottages up behind the mansion before it had been destroyed in a magical fire. My wall of crazy had been fairly crazy, but it had nothing on Aunt Cass's. There were maps, pages of old documents, property transfer records, wedding certificates, newspaper articles cut out, multiple colors of strings and pins, and for some reason, a black sock nailed to the wall.

"What am I looking for exactly?" I asked, trying to find a starting point to make sense of the chaos.

"Just look and tell me if you see anything," Aunt Cass said sounding positively giddy.

I moved around as I looked at the wall. Articles on men missing on Truer Island, wedding announcements, a hand-drawn timeline. Wait, what was that? I went back to the timeline. It was about the Moms and our dads. According to the timeline they had roughly met the Moms all at the same time, were married within two months of each other, had babies within eight months of each other, and then years later our fathers had left our Moms at roughly the same time.

"Is this timeline right? Is that you're talking about?" I asked.

"It is right, I think. Keep looking," Aunt Cass said.

I kept stepping across, trying to read all the articles and everything at once. Some of them seemed completely random, like an article about missing twins from the 1950s, and something called an Ice Cream Social Dance. I soon found the photo I'd only seen once before. It was Grandma April, Aunt Cass and Hattie Stern together, friends, all the same age. How is it that we hadn't investigated it the last time we saw it? Hattie Stern was at least twenty years younger than Aunt Cass, and yet here she was in the photo the same age.

"Why is Hattie twenty years younger than you?" I asked.

"That is an excellent question. Keep looking," Aunt Cass said. I eventually found a big blank space in the middle of the wall. Dotted all around it were articles about missing men, some who had vanished on Truer Island, others in Harlot Bay and in the surrounding towns. I turned to Aunt Cass and pointed at the big space.

"Is something missing here?" I asked.

Aunt Cass nodded, grinning at me. "I think it's *someone* who is missing. I've never seen this before even though *I* made the wall. Whatever it is that's been holding us, pushing me down for all these decades, it's getting weaker."

Hattie Stern had been the one to tell me she suspected there was a spell cast on me. Aunt Cass had said she had felt something pushing on her for years on end and I knew what she meant. I'd struggled against it sometimes myself, or so I thought. Whatever the spell was, if it existed at all, it was subtle and devious. Sometimes I would find myself thinking I should investigate but then end up in front of the television having had that desire slip out of my mind. It was easy to forget things, to let them slip. Was the spell really growing weaker?

"What does this mean though?" I asked Aunt Cass.

"It means that once our magic is back, we train hard. Your Mom is eager to get out to the island. But I think we should wait a little while, train as hard as we can, and then the seven of us go out there and kick britches!" Aunt Cass said.

"Britches?"

"Yeah, I'm assuming they didn't have pants back then, so logically... she'd be wearing britches right? If it really is her, Marguerite Torrent?"

"I can't remember what she was wearing when I saw her in the past. What do britches look like anyway?" I commented, turning around again to face the wall. I wanted to study it some more, but it was not to be. Aunt Cass tapped me on the shoulder and pointed to the door.

"Alright off you go. I have work to do, but it's not going to be long, Harlow," she said.

"Okay, fine, but I want to come down here and have another proper look," I said.

"Deal, now get out," Aunt Cass said and gently pushed me to the door. As I made my way back through the warm dark I could feel a kind of hope growing. It seemed that many things were ruined but also that something good was coming. By the time I reached the basement I was smiling.

"It's all gonna work out Grandma," I told her and then bolted up the stairs so I could go to work.

CHAPTER TWENTY

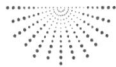

I was sitting up in my office thankful I was up on the second floor where no one could see in through the window. The national media had found me. They'd come to town once Sylvester Coldwell's body had been discovered. As usual, they had reported on the mysterious goings on in Harlot Bay, most the reporters barely hiding a smirk. Many of them were trying to connect the donuts found in Sylvester Coldwell's office and then strewn through the town up to the lighthouse with what happened to Sylvester not long after. They were all kinds of wild hypotheses with some of the less credible journalists speculating that the donuts were a warning from a famous New York Mafioso who owned a bakery.

When I arrived at work this morning I discovered it surrounded by news vans and waiting journalists. They'd staked the office out. Given Jonas's office was downstairs, some of them were hoping I could open the office and let them in; others were shouting questions at me. It seemed they'd discovered that I had had a run-in with Sylvester Coldwell in the past with an anonymous source reporting that myself and Carter had been seen arguing with Coldwell outside of a Council meeting a long time ago. I said no comment about fifty times as I made my way through the cameras and journalists shouting questions, got inside, locked the office and then went upstairs. I could still hear them down there, some of them shouting up questions, hoping they would get an answer, or that I would come over near the window.

I was pondering whether I'd have to call Sheriff Hardy so I could get out of my office later when a new email arrived. It was another video from "The Truth." This one was clearer than the first, and in it, I spotted Lazarus, goon number two with the goon appropriate name. He was driving up a dark road in a brown car that looked beat up. He got out of the car, and then the image panned up to show a blurry mansion in the background. As Lazarus began walking towards the mansion, the video abruptly cut off. The mansion may have been blurry, but I could recognize that building anywhere. It was the Coldwell Mansion where Sylvester Coldwell had lived along with his children, Richie and Natalia.

So what was this video showing? A man who was wanted for questioning going up to the Coldwell Mansion. There was a date on the video, it had been taken just yesterday.

With all the media attention on Harlot Bay there were news articles being produced every hour, but most of them were just recycling the same facts and speculation over and again. There were countless photographs of the pier or old file photographs of Sylvester Coldwell. I watched the video again and then made an abrupt decision. The Truth hadn't answered any of my questions about who they were or where they were getting these videos from, but perhaps their name was a clue as to what should happen. Perhaps the people of Harlot Bay deserved to know the truth. I still had access to the *Harlot Bay Times* website so I wrote up a short description advising that the *Harlot Bay Times* had received these two anonymous videos. Then I uploaded them to the front page and published them. All up it took over an hour considering how slow things were on the Internet for Harlot Bay, but soon they were up and I saw the view count begin to rise. It wasn't long after that, I heard shouting from down the street. One of the journalists.

"Harlow! Did you just publish the new video on the *Harlot Bay Times?*" a man yelled out. I decided I wasn't going to answer that. Let the media get into a frenzy. Hopefully, one of them would discover that the mansion in the background was Coldwell's and turn their attention to him. Thus far, August Coldwell had interviewed with the police over his brother's death, but not in the sense that he was arrested and taken in for questioning. He only released a short statement saying that he and his family were devastated by his brother's death and vowed to bring his killer to justice as well as continuing on his brother's good works. We assumed he meant the Harlot Bay Mall, which hadn't ceased construction.

I was sitting not doing anything much useful, mostly watching people make comments on the videos where some of the locals had already identified Coldwell's mansion in the background, when I felt a presence behind me. I whirled around in my chair to find Sylvester Coldwell standing there looking at my laptop screen. Most the time I saw Sylvester he was immaculately dressed, wearing a suit in perfect condition with not a hair out of place. Now he appeared disheveled, much the same way I encountered him when I had discovered him in his office, drinking heavily after Morris Sanderson had been discovered dead. Thankfully, Sylvester's aura wasn't looking any darker than usual. He was still a ghost, at least for the time being, and not some spiritual force of rage.

"Why is my home on there?" Coldwell demanded.

Ah good old Sylvester, that arrogance never left him.

I turned around and played the video. "An anonymous source sent it to me, so I've published it. I suspect that that man is one of the people behind the fire at Carter Wilkins' house," I said.

I had tried many times to talk with Sylvester about Carter Wilkins, but it had been almost useless. Most the time he claimed he didn't know who Carter was at all. Only one other time he'd said, "Oh, the journalist", but then immediately forgotten that he had said it.

"Was it Carter who stole the files from my office?" Coldwell asked.

Wow, this was new, he remembered the files? I decided to press on and go all the way.

"No, that was my cousins and me. We stole the files and we were very surprised to find us in them as well as Carter and other people in town. Can you tell us why Clifford and Lazarus were in there?" I asked.

"They were files on people I was keeping an eye on. Those two work for my brother," Sylvester said.

"Work for him how?"

"Who works with who?"

I groaned and stomped my foot on the ground.

"Come on, what do Clifford and Lazarus do for your brother?" I asked.

"Who are they?" Coldwell said.

I sighed. "Go watch over your children. Come back to me if they're in trouble," I said. It was the only way I could get rid of Sylvester: mention his children. He nodded and then slipped out through the door.

I went over to the window and peered out, expecting to find the street full of news vans, but surprisingly it was empty. All the journalists had gone elsewhere for the time being. I sent a message to Sheriff Hardy telling him that Clifford and Lazarus worked for August Coldwell, not Sylvester, then I locked up my office and bolted out of there before any of the journalists could come back. I had a fraught few moments in town as I was buying sandwiches when I swear I saw a journalist on the other side of the street, but then I got my food and got back to my car and drove out of Harlot Bay. As I was driving, I kept looking behind me, making sure that no one was following. I even looped around a few streets, went back and forth a few times, wishing that I had my magic so I could cast a concealment spell. Eventually, I was satisfied that I wasn't being tailed, so I parked in front of an old abandoned house and went inside. This was step one in the sneaking across to Jack scenario. Many of the homes in Harlot Bay had extra floors and hidden tunnels from back when the town was constantly under assault from pirates and also during Prohibition when it seemed that everyone had become criminals. This particular house had a basement and a fake wall. It led six houses away to another basement through a dusty corridor. I grabbed the flashlight and made my way down it, carrying the bag of food before emerging at the other end. I went upstairs into the darkened main entrance way. All the curtains were drawn so no one could see in. I went upstairs to find Jack sitting by a window that had been boarded up, except for a tiny slit. He was watching through it with a pair of high-powered binoculars.

"Lunch is here," I said. Jack turned around and gave me a half smile. I put the bag down and hugged him as hard as I could. I'd seen Jack worried before, but it had never been like this. His brother was in jail, the evidence didn't look good, and it seemed it had pushed Jack into some kind of cold professionalism. He'd set up surveillance on the Coldwell mansion, which was up the hill. Jack had even put video cameras in another house out on the other side of the mansion that would record anyone coming or going. It was illegal surveillance. Sheriff Hardy didn't know about it and I certainly wasn't going to tell him.

"I see you published a new video before," Jack said, once I pulled away from him.

I opened the bag of food and passed him a sandwich as well as a cold drink.

"The date on it said yesterday, and it was definitely Coldwell's mansion, did you see it?" I asked.

"There must be another road up around the back. It's a bit of a blind spot right now. We're going to get a camera on it though," Jack said before taking an enormous bite of his sandwich. We had our lunch and talked a little. We had chewed over the same topics a few times now, each of us picking up our scripts and playing our roles. Jack's position was that bad guys always slipped up eventually. There was always a hole somewhere and you just had to find it. He was convinced he would see something that he could use to expose Coldwell and save his brother.

I wasn't so sure but I kept those thoughts to myself. All of my research on August Coldwell had only brought up hints of wrongdoing. At most there had been a few lawsuits that had been settled. Carter had told me he had someone looking into August Coldwell from many years ago but now with him gone, that lead had gone cold. I stayed with Jack for a few hours, keeping silent warm company. It seemed incredible that only a few days ago we'd been under a lemon tree and he'd asked me to marry him. That we'd been at a school reunion dancing and drinking wine as though the world would never end. I'd even said to him that we would move in together but that had slipped by the by, all of our plans frozen.

Late in the afternoon I kissed Jack goodbye, went back through the secret tunnel, and then crept out to my car after making sure no one was watching it. As I headed back home I kept trying to feel for the magic, hoping that by stretching out, I could bring it back. All we needed was to cast a finding spell and we would be able to locate Clifford and Lazarus. Aunt Cass's ban on using Kira, or anyone else, was chafing on me, but I was trying to practice the art of patience. Now was not the time to go crazy and do something reckless. It was a time for calm, patient action. I shook my head to myself as I reached the mansion and parked. Calm, patient action? Did that sound like the Torrent witches at all?

CHAPTER TWENTY-ONE

Traveler was empty, which was perfect for Molly and Luce because they were plotting. I'd spent the morning working at home going through Carter's Coldwell files. I still hadn't found anything that would take down the Coldwell organization but in my defense there were a lot of files. I felt like I needed a complete team of forensic investigators to dig into this. I'd decided to work from home where I could have access to the files and also avoid the journalists who were still infesting the town.

I decided to risk a trip to town for lunch with my cousins because I had to get out of the house. Especially so with Adams moping about the place, complaining that he was wasting away to skin and bone on his diet of "plain" cat biscuits and "hose water". I still wasn't going to tell him the truth. He and Hugo had cost us quite a bit of money by eating all the food and drinking our wine. Let him mope for a few days. So I had driven into town and gone to *Traveler* to discover my two cousins conspiring over a tiny bottle.

"Check it out, Harlow, truth serum," Luce said, waving a tiny bottle at me.

"Did Aunt Cass make you some more?" I asked, slightly confused because Aunt Cass still didn't have all of her magic back.

"Nope, this is the one that I dropped in Molly's car ages ago. We decided to go searching for it and we found it!" Luce said.

A long time ago after Molly and Luce's coffee machine had been stolen, Aunt Cass had brewed up a bottle of truth serum for them. They'd held a party at *Traveler* inviting all of the builders and people who had worked on the renovation of *Traveler*. The plan was to give them doses of truth serum to see whether they had stolen the coffee machine. Unfortunately, things had gone slightly awry when Luce had dropped the entire bottle of truth serum into the bowl of punch. Suddenly there was a lot of truth being spoken and a *lot* of deep secrets revealed. The night had then gone further off the rails as I'd cast what was meant to be a spell to give people slight digestive discomfort so they would need to go home. Unfortunately, being a slip witch it had gone a little further than I had intended, and not everyone had made it home in time before having a terrible accident in their pants. Luce had managed to retrieve the bottle from the punch, but then later on had lost it in Molly's car.

I took a seat in the booth across from my cousins. Luce passed me the truth serum—there were still a few drops in the bottom.

"So what are you going to do with this?" I asked, tipping the bottle from side to side.

"Duh, we dose August Coldwell. We film him confessing to setting up Jonas and doing everything else," Molly said.

"Does that include confessing to sabotaging *Traveler*?" I asked.

"Maybe. If it comes up," Molly said.

I knew both my cousins were very concerned about Jonas

being falsely accused but the sabotage of *Traveler* had hit them hard, especially financially. Despite the fact they had been open for a while now they'd barely had any customers. The tour buses that came through town and traditionally came to them were now all going over to The Magic Bean. Molly and Luce had even lost Blake, their scruffy guitarist, to them.

"So what do you say, Harlow? Are you in?" Luce asked.

"In what? Do you have a plan?"

Luce stood up and began pacing around.

"Well we know August Coldwell is living up at the Coldwell Mansion. Jack's been watching the place, so he knows who's coming and going. I say the three of us sneak in, tie August Coldwell up, get the video camera, dose him with the serum, and voilà! We're done," she said, giving a little bow at the end.

It definitely wasn't the worst plan my cousins had come up with but then again, it wasn't the best either. Many of the times we'd gone to break and enter into places it had gone terribly wrong and we were still without our magic.

"And what happens when one of us gets stressed and donuts start falling from the ceiling in front of August Coldwell?" I asked.

"Oh, I know, we'll have some drinks in the car before we go," Molly said.

"So we're going to be *drunk* and tying up August Coldwell after breaking in and then filming him?" I asked.

Molly stuck her bottom lip out, pouting. "Fine, maybe the plan needs a little work," she said.

"Oh no," Luce groaned reading something off her phone.

"What is it?" I asked.

"Hugo is gone," she said.

Shock ran through me. Oh Goddess, I'd been "starving"

Adams with his plain cat biscuits and hose water. Surely he hadn't...

"Did Adams eat him?" I asked.

Luce frowned at me. "No, Adams wouldn't eat Hugo. They're friends. He just told me that he's caught a flight to England, that he needs to 'return home' or whatever. Apparently, he's going to be landing at Heathrow, according to his email," she said.

"Isn't he from *here* though? I mean, I don't think whoever got those mice would have bothered importing them from England just to sabotage a coffee shop in North Carolina," I said.

"I know! And how did he even get an email account?" Luce said.

I took a breath and let it go. Okay, there was possibly a talking mouse out in the world. Who knows, maybe it would wear off once he left Harlot Bay?

"Dear Hugo, so sorry to see you go. Hope you find what you're looking for. Please visit anytime you want. Love, Luce," Luce said aloud as she typed away on her phone.

"Well at least that's one less thing to worry about," Molly said.

Luce whirled on our cousin. "You never liked Hugo did you? I bet you were involved in it. Did you buy him his ticket to Heathrow?" she said, pointing an accusing finger.

"That is an absurd accusation. If we didn't need this truth serum, I would drink it right now and prove to you I had nothing to do with it," Molly said.

"Lucky for you we need it then," Luce said in a level tone.

The standoff was broken by the bell above the door jingling. We turned around to see Bella Bing walking in followed closely by Ru.

Bella wasn't dressed in her standard I'm-a-movie-star-trying-to-remain-inconspicuous-by-wearing-a-ridiculous-amount-of-expensive-things costume. She actually sort of looked like a normal person for once. She had a pair of jeans and a green wool sweater, no jewelry, and minimal makeup. That didn't stop her from looking us over.

"Still no customers at *Traveler*? How surprising," she said in a flat tone.

I was getting ready to snark back at her and I could see Luce working up a response as well, but then Molly leaped up out of the booth and waved both of us down.

"Thanks for coming Bella. I really wanted to talk to you," Molly said. Bella crossed her arms and frowned.

"Well fine, go ahead and talk then," she said.

Molly looked around at us and then at Ru, biting her lip.

"Let's just go out the front for a minute, just us," she said. Bella nodded and followed Molly out the front of *Traveler*. Ru stayed inside, looking out the front window with her flawless green eyes.

We couldn't hear what Molly was saying, but soon both she and Bella were crying and hugging. It went on for about five minutes of them out there blubbering in public, their eyes turning red, tears running down their faces. At first I tensed up not knowing what was going to happen, but eventually I relaxed. It was Molly's apology to Bella for what had happened in the past and it looked like it was going well, or I guessed it was. There was more crying and hugging outside and then eventually they both came in. Bella's eyes were red and swollen and her nose was snotty. She looked about as far away from being a movie star as anyone could be.

"I'm so sorry I was mean Luce," Bella said and gave her a quick hug. When she pulled away, I saw the front of Luce's shirt was wet with tears and a little bit of snot. Before I could get up from the booth, Bella dived on me and gave me a very damp hug. I patted her on the back and then it wasn't long after that before she was gone, taking Ru with her. Molly sat down on the other side of the booth and grabbed a few napkins to wipe away her tears. Then she let out a long sigh of relief.

"They felt really good," she said.

CHAPTER TWENTY-TWO

"That's it! I can't take it anymore!" Kira declared. She rushed over to the front door of *The Cozy Cat* and locked it.

"What are you doing? People won't be able to get in," Peta protested.

"Okay listen up, Peta Peta pumpkin eater. We haven't had a single customer all day, so one it's not a big deal; two, I'm tired of you moping and I have magic, so let's do something. I can track people down. I can brew potions. The Torrents are out of commission right now, but I'm not. I'm tired of coming to work and seeing you moping around. What can we do to help your boyfriend? Let's do it," Kira said. To highlight her point she let a ball of golden light erupt from her hand that transformed into the image of a dog as it leaped through the air. It hit the ground and burst into tiny sparkles that shimmered away.

Oh boy... I was really hoping I would avoid something like this.

"I don't know what we can do. Can you find the people who might have gone into Jonas's house?" Peta asked.

"That is an excellent question! Harlow, don't you have a photo or something of them?" Kira asked.

"How do you know that?" I asked.

"I don't know, I must've heard it somewhere," Kira said, pointing her finger next door to *Traveler*.

I sighed. Luce or Molly talking too much.

"Um yeah, I do have a photo of them and their names, but I don't think you should be involved," I said.

"Why not?" Peta asked.

"Yeah, why not? It's just a finding spell. Maybe we can find these people, take them down," Kira said.

Ugh! I was going to have to say things I didn't want to say.

"It's just that Aunt Cass promised your Grandma that you wouldn't get involved."

Kira snorted. "That's *adorable*. I decide the things I'm involved in, not my Grandma. Now do you have the photo or not?" she said.

"Please, Harlow?" Peta asked.

I sighed again and tried to think of a way out of this, but I just couldn't. Peta had opened *The Cozy Cat* again but it was true that she'd been despondent. There'd barely been any customers, so she didn't even have work to take her mind off the fact that Jonas was still sitting in a cell down at the Harlot Bay police station. I told Peta that as soon as our magic returned that we would help her, but thus far it hadn't and time was dragging on. But then again, although Aunt Cass had said not to get Kira involved, it wasn't exactly my promise to Hattie Stern now was it? It was *Aunt Cass* promising Hattie, not *me*.

Besides, it was just a finding spell. As soon as it went to a location we would call Sheriff Hardy and he'd go and arrest those men.

"Okay, fine, you can do a finding spell. I have their photos on my phone," I said. I'd taken photos of the files just in case I came across the men or needed to show the photos to anyone. I doubled checked that the front door was locked while Kira had a look at the photos, memorizing the features of the two men. Then she put the phone down on the counter, slowed her breathing and a moment later whispered, "Find". Unlike Aunt Cass who merely produced a tiny spark of light that flared away, Kira immediately produced a golden ball of light. It would only be visible to witches, so Peta couldn't see it. The light began drifting towards the front door.

"It's moving, let's go," Kira commanded. We rushed out of *The Cozy Cat*, Peta locking it behind her and jumped in my ancient car. The ball was already traveling down the road picking up speed. After a heart-stopping moment where the car wouldn't start, we finally got going and managed to catch up with the ball which was weaving its way through town.

"Do you have your phone ready to call the sheriff?" Kira asked Peta.

"Right here. As soon as we find them I'm going to call," she said.

We followed the light into what I guess you would call one of the lower socio-economic areas of Harlot Bay. There were plenty of streets like this one in Harlot Bay where entire houses had been abandoned and were merely sitting there marking off time until someone bought them for next to nothing, or they collapsed from neglect. Where we were heading was out to the edge of Harlot Bay and a particularly rundown part of town. It wasn't long before the ball began to slow, moving up onto the sidewalk and into the rundown front gardens of the houses along the street. It was then that we began to lose sight of it. Many of the homes had huge overgrown gardens filled with trees and weeds and other bushes. I stopped the car and we all jumped out, running across onto the sidewalk so we could keep up with the ball of light. It briefly crossed my mind that we must've looked strange to anyone who might be watching as we were all still wearing our Cozy Cat 1950s uniforms.

"Do you see it, Harlow? Where has it gone?" Kira asked.

"It's right there," I said. The ball was drifting into a particularly large overgrown front yard. We slowed as we approached. We certainly didn't want to go walking into any house where the two thugs might be staying. But we needed to be sure exactly where the ball was going. For all we knew it could be heading over the back fence.

"Just be ready to throw a fireball or something if it comes to it," I whispered to Kira. I opened a very squeaky front gate and we went into a gigantic overgrown front yard. The golden ball was moving down the side of the house and picking up speed again.

We moved over to near the side of the house but stood there, unwilling to go any further.

"Let's just wait and see where it goes," I said, putting out a warning hand to stop Kira and Peta going any further. I heard the sound of an old wooden window opening somewhere in the distance. But I was too focused on watching the golden ball, trying to see where it was going. It was then I heard Kira let out a cry beside me before she slumped to the ground, a small dart sticking out of her back. I whirled around to see a long barrel sticking out of an upstairs window of the house, pointing directly at me. There was a stab of pain in my chest and then I was on the ground. The world was swimming and then I saw Peta topple over before everything went black.

CHAPTER TWENTY-THREE

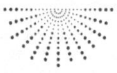

The stars are beautiful, I thought, as I lay on my back and watched them. They were twinkling gently and so I lay and stared at them for a while, feeling warm and content. Eventually that contentment began to fade, the sensations began to get through to my sleepy mind. The ground was hard... no it wasn't ground, it was concrete and it was hard and cold. I tried to move, but my arms and legs were stuck. As I tried to work out what was happening I heard a man's voice nearby.

"This one's awake," he said.

"I told you the doses were too high," said another voice.

"Turn her over," said a cold voice. I saw a face above me and then felt someone touch me and push me from my back onto my side. The world swam, ground and sky interchanging itself and when it all finally stopped moving I saw three men in front of me. Two were... I knew them but from what? Oh right, the files. Behind them was a third man, his face half in shadow. He looked familiar.

"Sylvester? What are you doing here?" I called out. It felt like I was talking through a mouth of cotton wool.

The man in the shadows stepped forward into a harsh yellow light.

"My brother is dead, and you will be too if you don't answer my questions," August Coldwell said. It took a moment for the fear to hit me but when it did, it was like a sledgehammer to my heart. Cold adrenaline burst through me, and the final remnants of whatever I'd been shot with seemed to evaporate in an instant. I had been with Kira and Peta. We were trying to track down the thugs and I'd been shot was something, obviously a sedative of some kind. I drew another breath to let out a scream but then suddenly one of the thugs was in front of me, pointing a gun at my head.

"Be quiet now, or something bad will happen to your friends," he said. It was Lazarus, the tall one. Over to the side the other one Clifford, chubby with spiky blond hair, was watching us.

"What do you want?" I managed to say, although fear was clenching my insides. I saw Kira and Peta were nearby, their arms bound behind them and their feet tied just like me. We were all lying on a concrete slab somewhere in the dark with a harsh light shining down around us. It took a moment for me to work out where we were but when I did I almost screamed again. It was the mall construction site. Far away from where anyone could help us. My gaze went over to the side where there was a large pit dug out and beside it a parked concrete mixer.

"Oh Goddess, no," I moaned. I could see two bodies already in the bottom of the pit, hands tied behind them and feet bound.

August glanced across at the pit and then back to me. His expression was flat and cold, inhuman.

"My niece and nephew, they're of no use to me," he said. I saw Lazarus go walking off into the darkness. The night was quiet, and all I could hear was the thudding of my heart and somewhere in the distance, the faint sound of traffic. I heard the sound of a trunk being opened and then slammed shut again.

"Kira, are you okay," I called out.

I had no magic. I couldn't reach for it, but if Kira could wake up perhaps she could save us.

"I think Lazarus used too high a dose on your friend. She might wake up before she goes into the pit," Clifford said.

August waved at him to be quiet and walked closer to me.

"Where are my brother's files? Who has been sending you videos of my mansion? And where are the files that Carter Wilkins gave you?" August asked.

I was terrified, but I knew the only play here that might lead us to safety was to delay things long enough so that Kira could wake up. She was smaller than Peta and me, so presumably the sedative would work for longer. If I could delay things long enough, perhaps she would awake.

"Your brother's files are at my house up in the ceiling," I said. My teeth were beginning to chatter, the cold of the concrete leaching into my bones.

"Well, that was easy. Who's been sending you the videos?"

"I don't know, they just call themselves The Truth. I get them by email," I said. And then I did scream when Lazarus came walking back into the light dragging two unconscious figures with him. It was Molly and Luce, their hands bound behind them, their feet tied. The world spun, and I tasted blood in my mouth. Someone had hit me. Through the pain, I saw Lazarus dump Molly and Luce next to Peta and Kira. Thank the Goddess, they were both still breathing.

"Please, please, please, don't hurt them. Please," I said, begging.

"Where are Carter Wilkins' files?" August asked.

Despite the taste of blood in my mouth and the pain and

the fear that was running through me, I knew I couldn't answer because then what reason would he have to keep me alive. Lazarus was already lingering over near the concrete mixer evidently getting prepared for the next stage in the evening.

"Why did you kill your own brother?" I asked. I saw Clifford move towards me and noticed he had a smear of blood on his shoe. He must've kicked me. August waved him back.

"Do you have any proof that I killed my brother?" August said. It was then that I saw the ghostly figure of Sylvester Coldwell. He came walking out of the dark, his eyes fixed on his brother.

"Ask him what happened to my rabbit. Ask him what happened to Barnabas," Sylvester said.

It was a crazy risk, but I had to do anything I could to delay what was going to happen next.

"What happened to Barnabas?" I asked.

August opened his eyes wide in surprise and then stepped back from me, a strange expression on his face.

"Did you interview my brother? I always thought you were enemies. But did he tell you things? Did he tell you lies about me?"

"Ask him why our father locked him in the hurt cupboard," Sylvester said. In the harsh light of the building lamps, Sylvester's aura appeared golden to me, but I could see it darkening.

"Why did your father lock you in the hurt cupboard?" I asked.

August let out a sigh and looked at Clifford and Lazarus who were watching our interaction.

"This is cute, but I asked you a clear question. Where are Carter Wilkins' files? If you don't give me an answer I'm going to shoot one of them," he said.

I saw Sylvester step forward and swing a fist at his

brother, but he was a ghost. As soon as it connected he bounced away, sliding to a halt over near the pit. He looked over and saw his children, unconscious or dead, I didn't know, and fell to his knees and started sobbing ghostly tears.

"Carter's files are in my house as well. They're not even hidden, you can just go and get them," I said.

August nodded and then gave a signal to Lazarus who switched on the concrete mixer. The machine roared and then quieted down, idling.

"I was just going to kill you all, but because you've been so helpful, I think I'll leave you alive while my friends pour the concrete on you," August said.

I went numb as Lazarus and Clifford came forward and dragged Molly and Luce into the pit. When they returned, Lazarus handed August the small bottle of truth serum.

"One of them had this on them," he said. Then he and Clifford dragged Kira over to the pit.

"Is this poison? Those two were hiding outside my mansion. Was that the plan, to break in and poison me?" he asked.

"It's not poison," I said. I was trying to get my hands free, trying to move without him seeing it, but the bonds were too tight.

"Then you won't mind drinking it then will you," he said. He opened the bottle and came over. I opened my mouth rather than have him try to force it, and he tipped the truth serum down my throat. It tasted sweet, and within a moment warmth spread through my body.

"Your brother's ghost is watching you," I said, eager to talk and tell the truth.

"Sure, whatever you say," August said.

"He's the one that told me about Barnabas. He is just over there by the pit crying over his children. I'm trying to delay you because then Kira will wake up and use her magic to free us," I said. I could feel myself trying to *not* say these things, but the potion was compelling me.

"Magic, wow, that sounds great," August said sarcastically. He looked over to where Clifford and Lazarus were rearranging the unconscious bodies of Richie, Natalia, Molly, Luce, Peta, and Kira.

"Make sure no one's stacked on top of another. We want this to be a nice smooth surface," he said.

"If I had my magic you'd be dead," I said.

"Hey, these two are starting to wake up finally," Lazarus said from the pit.

"As much fun as it would be to wait, let's get this done with so I can go home to sleep," August said. Lazarus and Clifford came over and picked me up off the ground by my arms. The warmth of the truth serum had wiped away my fear almost entirely.

"You'd better hope my Aunt Cass never finds out that it was you. She'll flay the skin from your bones for this," I threatened.

"We'll get her next then," Lazarus grunted, and then Clifford laughed. They lay me down in the pit next to Kira. Her eyelids were fluttering. Sometimes she would open them before falling back into unconsciousness. The two men climbed out of the pit and walked over near the concrete mixer. It had a large sluice on the end of it that the concrete would come pouring out of and I knew all they had to do was hit the button and all of us would be drowned. I wriggled forward closer to Kira and tapped my head against hers.

"Kira, wake up," I called out. I heard the concrete mixer rev as one of the men did something. I couldn't get any purchase to hit Kira any harder hoping to wake her up so I did the only thing I could and leaned forward and bit her lip as hard as I could. Kira's eyes jerked open, and she pulled away from me, a streak of blood running down her face.

"They're going to kill us! Fireball now," I commanded.

I don't know if it made sense to the scared teenager. There was no fireball though. There was just a tremendous lurch in the magic, and suddenly it was back. I saw Molly and Luce gasp awake as the return of the magic wiped away the sedative. As the magic returned so did my fear, and along with it came rage. I was off the ground in an instant somehow tearing free from my bonds with supernatural strength. I saw August shouting to his men who were drawing weapons, but it was a mere flick of my hand to fling their guns away and press them against the concrete mixer where they couldn't move.

I blinked, tasting blood in my mouth and then all around me I saw them. The dark slip witches I had seen once long ago. They were urging me on, and this time there would be no cat to bite me on the leg to bring me back. I let a surge of magic go across into Sylvester Coldwell, and suddenly he was solid and real. He stood up from the ground where he had been weeping and walked towards his brother.

"You murdered me, you were going to murder my children, and you murdered my pet rabbit," he said.

"I didn't, I wasn't," August said. Sylvester lunged forward, his fingers passing through his brother's chest and stopped his heart. August fell backward, dead on the ground. Sylvester looked at me and then let out a sigh of relief before breaking into pieces and vanishing.

I heard voices calling me. My cousins? Kira? Whatever it was, it didn't matter. I still had Clifford and Lazarus in my grasp. I pulled some of their life away and pushed it into August, restarting his heart. I wanted him alive, so I could enjoy what was going to come next. The voices around me faded. Even the dark slip witches were gone, and all I could see was August Coldwell and his two thugs. What merciless fury I would rain down upon them. Then I felt someone touch my hand. I went to swat whoever it was away, but they were immovable. I took my gaze away from August Coldwell and turned my head to see a man with eyes that hovered between blue and green. He was talking to me. Nothing he said made sense. Who was Harlow? Why was he saying he loved me?

The cold dark fury that had taken hold of me was replaced with confusion and then a breath later it all came back to me. I was Harlow. This was Jack. We were in love and going to get married. The roaring in my ears faded away, and I could hear him.

"Harlow, I love you, don't do this," he pleaded with me. I looked at him properly for the first time and let out a sigh, letting all of the anger wisp away.

"I'm here Jack, it's me," I said. Behind him, I saw flashing lights, and I could hear the police sirens. Out of the dark came Sheriff Hardy and his men, rushing across to grab the two thugs and August, some of them jumping into the pit to help free the rest of the captives. I wrapped my arms around Jack and put my head on his shoulder. The anger was being replaced by a deep and bone weary tiredness. Still, that wasn't enough to prevent me starting when I saw a familiar face walk out of the darkness.

It was Carter. He was alive.

CHAPTER TWENTY-FOUR

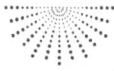

"All I'm saying is if it was the 1950s I would have dated you so hard," Jack said giving me a sideways look from the driver's seat of his truck.

"This old thing? You like my uniform?" I said, running my fingers along the hem of my Cozy Cat waitress outfit.

"I adore that outfit," Jack said and winked at me.

I smiled and touched him on the arm. The world wasn't broken anymore.

The dark night in the pit of the Harlot Bay mall construction site was two weeks in the past. Finally, the media frenzy that had flooded Harlot Bay had died down and all the national media had gone home, which meant today I was going take a quick trip past my office to see what sort of state it was in before I went to work at *The Cozy Cat*.

The national media had done a full two weeks on the goings-on in Harlot Bay, but eventually even they'd gotten sick of chewing over the same facts and had departed.

The first amazing fact: Carter was alive. He'd been working in a back room when the smoke alarms in his house went off. He had seen his partner Constance go out the front as he had bolted out the back escaping over the fence. It was then that he had seen the two thugs, Clifford and Lazarus, waiting in a car around the corner to ensure that their arson had gone off successfully. Carter had hidden in a nearby abandoned house during the day and then at night started his surveillance on August Coldwell, Lazarus and Clifford. He had been the one sending me the videos hoping that I would publish them on the *Harlot Bay Times* website. I was certainly very relieved to see Carter and so was his partner Constance, although I heard that she had smacked him one in the face a second after hugging him for allowing her to believe that he'd been killed in the house fire. Carter had every excuse in the world, and I didn't think he was wrong. He believed that if he revealed he'd survived the fire that there would shortly be another attack on his life, and so it was better to go undercover to try to expose the Coldwell family. I could see his point, but I also agreed with Constance slapping him.

The two thugs, Clifford and Lazarus, had turned on their boss with startling speed. There was no amount he could pay them to prevent them revealing the truth of what they'd been ordered to do. There was also the weight of physical evidence pouring in. One of them, Clifford, had been using a gun that was matched to the one used to kill Morris Sanderson. The other, Lazarus, had a gun that was matched to other crimes in other states, all associated with August Coldwell-backed projects. The men had confessed that they'd been ordered to kill Morris Sanderson and to sabotage *Traveler*, the *Torrent Mansion Bed and Breakfast*, and to firebomb the *Chili Challenge*, although Clifford blamed Lazarus and he blamed Clifford in return. It wasn't clear who pulled the trigger on Morris, both men claiming they'd only gone along because they were scared and in too deep, and it had been the other who had been the criminal to commit the act.

August Coldwell's plan had been quite simple in the end:

He knew that his brother had had trouble with the Torrent family in the past and knew of his opposition to the free rent program. He wanted to take control of the mall project, and so his first step was to sabotage *Traveler* and the bed and breakfast and firebomb the *Chili Challenge*, hoping to draw negative attention to his brother. He also ordered Morris Sanderson killed, knowing that he had been a friend of his brother's since childhood. It had come out in the weeks since that August and Sylvester had faced horrific abuse at the hands of their father. Morris's widow described how Sylvester and Morris had been friends and Sylvester had sought solace in Morris's home ever since they were children. It was strange hearing that side of Sylvester Coldwell's life. Every interaction I had had with him over my life had been negative. When Morris's death and the sabotage hadn't attracted the attention required to shut the project down so August could take it over, he'd gone a step further and burnt down Carter Wilkins' house, knowing that he'd had many conflicts with his brother Sylvester. And when that didn't work? He'd finally taken off the kid gloves and ordered his brother killed. The final stage in August's plan was to have Richie and Natalia simply disappear along with anyone else he considered was causing him problems. If me, Kira and Peta hadn't gone to the house on that day, Richie and Natalia would have vanished that night, never to be seen again.

The official story, according to the police, was that the two thugs had grabbed Molly and Luce so they could use them to threaten me for information. The real story, which was not released, was that Molly and Luce had been hiding out over near Coldwell's with their bottle of truth serum looking for their moment. My cousins, Goddess bless them, had lied as much as they could about that to the Moms, and the Moms had grudgingly accepted their explanation.

August was alive too although it was unknown whether

they would be able to get any useful information out of him. It was said he kept muttering just one word to himself over and again: Barnabas.

Jonas had been released, of course, once Clifford and Lazarus's confession had come forth. He'd been drugged so the gun could be planted in his house after they wrapped his hands around it to plant his fingerprints on it.

Now the media had finally left town, Jonas and Jack were back at work finishing up the Governor's mansion.

In amongst all this the original Big Pie Bakery had been rebuilt but not yet opened. The Moms were looking at moving back soon, with the possibility of keeping both sites open. There were still no bookings at the *Torrent Mansion Bed and Breakfast* thanks to the sabotage, but the Moms were still hopeful for the future. Mom had been pushing somewhat for us to go out to the mansion on Truer Island, but unfortunately she, Aunt Ro and Aunt Freya still didn't have their magic back. It was just Aunt Cass, me, Molly and Luce.

Kira was back with her Grandma and last we heard apparently grounded for the rest of time. I had received just a single message from Kira: *What a crazy night, H-bomb, thanks for biting me.*

Jack and I pulled up in front of my office and got out of his truck. I walked up the stairs and opened my office door, dreading what I would find. Sure enough the entire place was covered in dust, seemingly an inch thick.

"Adams?" Jack called out as soon as we stepped into the room. I looked down beside the sofa where I saw a very familiar looking black tail.

"Adams what are you doing here?" I said and stepped across to take a look. The little black cat was down by the side of the sofa eating something.

"Nothing. I'm not doing anything," Adams said through a mouthful of something.

"You're eating something," I said.

"I thought you were at *The Cozy Cat* today!" Adams said and bolted behind the sofa.

"Is that a crumpet? Where did you get a crumpet from?"

"None of your business!" Adams called out. He ran away from the sofa and headed for some boxes stacked at the front of my office.

"If I see you with a cup of tea you're in big trouble mister!" I called out as Adams disappeared behind the boxes

"He went to England didn't he?" Jack said.

"He got strawberry preserve on my sofa," I said, inspecting the side of it.

"Is um... John here at all? Can I sit down?" Jack asked pointing towards the sofa.

"Sure, go right ahead—" I said before a memory hit me with such force that I had to sit down.

It was of John Smith in this very office, watching television, telling me that his name was Jack. Immediately after that he'd seen the news report about the hunt for suspects in the *Chili Challenge* firebombing case and had bolted out of the office with me close behind him. He'd then been hit by a car and been flung off into the distance and hadn't seen him since. In all the chaos of that time, I'd completely forgotten that he had told me his name was Jack.

"John, Jack, he said, he was right there," I blurted out, not making any sense.

My laptop had been left at the office and was covered in dust. Thankfully today it didn't take long to start up.

When it did though, a shock ran through me. My email opened and there was a message.

Harlow, I know it has been years but I have been thinking a lot about you lately. I know I've been gone and you might not want to but I'd like to come visit, if I could.

- *Dad*

I couldn't... it was too much on top of everything else. So I did what Torrent Witches are best at—I lied to myself, telling myself nothing was there and closed my email.

I began searching for Jack Smith. What other clues had I been given? He'd done acapella in the past. I kept searching and then the Internet dragged up a photo attached to an article. I swear my mouth literally fell open as I saw a very young John Smith. Underneath the photograph, it didn't say John Smith though, it said Jack Twist. But even that wasn't what was causing my shock. It had been a swing dancing competition and John—or Jack—and his partner had won. The young girl beaming from the photo with her arm wrapped around John was none other than Aunt Cass. At the bottom of the photo it said "Jack Twist and Talica Moore win again!"

Jack leaned over my shoulder and looked at the screen.

"Was your aunt using a fake name?" he said.

"It's a witch thing," I murmured.

It felt like the universe was spinning. John Smith and Aunt Cass had met before. The last time I could remember was at the Harlot Bay Museum when we were sneaking in trying to steal a compass. They'd acted like they hadn't known each other.

On another occasion, again when I'd been wearing 1950s swing style clothing, John had approached me in a park and called me Talica Moore, mistaking me for someone else.

How could this be?

I was fumbling for my phone getting ready to call home. I knew Aunt Cass was there today because in the morning she told me she was going to be planting more chili crops up behind the mansion. As I finally grabbed my phone it rang in my hand. It was Mom and she was frantic.

"Harlow, I need you at home right away. It's Aunt Cass. She went under the mansion. I think she's in trouble!"

The panic and sheer terror in her voice were like an icicle in my heart. I shot up from my chair so fast that I knocked it over and Jack jumped back.

"What happened, is she okay?" I called out.

"Just get here right away!" Mom yelled and then hung up.

The drive back to the mansion was a blur. I was in my Cozy Cat uniform and kept digging my nails into my knees. Jack was driving fast, his hands gripping the steering wheel, his body tense. He skidded to a stop out the front of the mansion and Mom opened the front door. She was crying. I ran inside and she grabbed me in a fierce hug.

"Quick this way," she cried.

"What is it Dalilah?" Jack asked, but she didn't answer him. She ran into the house, through the kitchen, down the stairs and under the mansion and we followed. She didn't even bother grabbing a flashlight, so I cast a ball of light to drift above us as we chased along behind her. In her frantic haste, Mom outran us down a corridor.

"Wait Mom, wait!" I yelled out. I heard a distant door slam, but she didn't stop. I turned a corner and then came to a halt so fast that Jack crashed into the back of me. There in the dark, glowing with a blue nimbus, was John Smith. Or was it Jack Twist? He had a red mark over his heart and a streak of light that went up and around his head. The last time I'd seen him like this the red around his head had been deep and dark like a crown. Now I could barely see it at all. His eyes widened when he saw me.

"Talica, I knew I'd find you here!" he called out. He took a step towards me and then must've realized that I wasn't who he thought I was.

"Is that John?" Jack said.

Wait, *he* could see him now? Was my magic leaking?

"Harlow, where's Cass, I need her right now," he said. He lunged forward and grabbed me by the arms and for a moment they felt solid and real before he let me go.

"I don't know where she is. Mom said she's in trouble!" I cried.

John rushed past me. Before he disappeared around the corner he stopped and looked back at me.

"I'm not dead, Harlow. I remember, you need to come find me," he called out before he vanished into the dark.

"We need to stop and think," Jack said but he was cut off. It was Mom. She was screaming in pain. I took off through the dark, my little light barely able to keep up. I was leaping around holes in the floor running towards the sound of my mother's voice. Jack was right behind me. Suddenly there was a door in front of us and I opened it and we fell through, the drop on the other side was about two feet down to cold wet stone. I landed hard and felt like I had the breath knocked out of me, scratching up my knees and hands. Jack crashed to the ground beside me. As soon as we went through the door the screaming ceased. I rolled over and sat up and saw Mom standing in the doorway. Her face was blank. Up around her head like a red crown was a weaving of light.

"What's that on her head?" Jack asked.

"It's a spell. She's bewitched," I said. Before I could get to my feet Mom slammed the door shut and then it vanished, leaving only a cold rock wall behind. We got to our feet and looked around. We were in some cold, underground cavern, the ground wet stone. My little light wasn't strong enough to illuminate the area. I sent it bobbing away from me to see whether I could find an exit. It lit up the wall and then what appeared to be a giant chunk of orange amber. Inside it I could see the shape of a man trapped within. The light drifted on. Beside it was another chunk of amber, but this one held a skeleton, barely visible. Beyond that I saw other older chunks of amber, faint shapes within.

"We need to get out of here," I whispered. My terror was real and complete and I had a sudden knowledge of exactly where we were. It was the mansion out on Truer Island. This is where the witch, my ancestor, Marguerite Torrent had made her lair. I grabbed Jack by the arm and we walked a few steps together, following the light, when I felt a powerful spell grip me. I turned, unable to control my limbs, and found myself marching up a slope that led to a cold stone platform. My small light followed me and I could see Jack was marching beside me, his movements jerky. We came to a halt upon the dais. In front of me the dark of the cave was complete, a black night without stars.

And then, the blackness moved. It took shape, a woman, one I had seen before. The one who looked like me.

"Marguerite," I managed to say before the spell grabbed me and froze my tongue. She stepped out of the darkness. She was like a mirror to me, but perhaps a few years older. She was smiling but I also saw she was shaking, perhaps with the effort of holding the spell. She stepped onto the platform in front of us and then turned her gaze to Jack.

"I will give you the choice I have given others," she said. Her voice echoed through the room, seeming stretched over time, ethereal and faint.

"Step into the darkness and join me and *you* shall be forgotten forevermore. But your beloved Harlow will survive and live a long and happy life," she said.

I tried to scream but I could not move a muscle. I could see Jack out of the corner of my eye, straining against his bonds.

Then Marguerite turned her gaze to me. I became aware of the aura surrounding her. It was as black as ink, with the slightest of golden sparkles drifting through it.

"Or you may abandon her and I will take Harlow instead. She will be forgotten forevermore but you, dearest Jack, shall live," she whispered.

I could feel the magic around me. It was swirling as though I was in the eye of a hurricane. Her magic was deep and dark and bitter, and I had felt it before.

But I could not move, could not cast a spell. I strained again and then felt a lurch as I slipped. But it was no magic to help me. It was a memory that appeared unbidden in my mind. I was in a clearing, Aunt Cass on the ground in front of me, her eyes as black as marbles in the grip of a prophecy.

"The guard dies. The tourist betrayed. The sister bewitched. The friend frozen. All forgotten, all lost. Once again, once again."

Where was that from? Was this real or some trick of the magic cast by Marguerite to distract me?

"Choose," Marguerite said. The magic let go.

He was so fast I could not stop him. Without hesitation, Jack plunged forward into the darkness, sacrificing himself. I reached for him, the tip of my finger brushing his shoulder. I went to scream but then the darkness rushed forward and there was nothing more.

CHAPTER TWENTY-FIVE

"I told you not to tell him to come!" I heard Aunt Cass say with a liberal dose of snark.

"Well he deserved to know! I was frozen for twenty years, you know, because of that."

What was happening? Where was I? Was that Hattie?

"Oh you love it, being younger than everyone now. That's what you get for interfering," Aunt Cass said.

"That's what I got for trying to protect you!" Hattie snapped back.

"Will you two shut up, I'm trying to concentrate," said another voice. I opened my eyes. I was on the floor of the basement underneath the kitchen. Standing around me were Aunt Cass, Hattie Stern and Grandma April. She was alive, unfrozen, her hands out above me crackling with magic. Lines were appearing on her face, her hair graying as years caught up with her.

"Oh, you're one to talk. You couldn't have given us a clue?" Aunt Cass snapped.

"As soon as I found out I had about a minute to decide so quit your complaining," Grandma snapped back.

I tried to get up from the floor but I seemed to have no strength.

I saw Grandma looking down at me.

"There will be great forces opposing you. You're going to need to be sneaky and sly," she said, a gentle twinkle in her eye.

"Shouldn't be a problem, she is a Torrent witch after all," Hattie said.

Strangely enough it sounded like a compliment.

"Damn right she is," Aunt Cass said proudly.

"Now," Grandma whispered.

I staggered to my feet, the spell roaring around me. It was unbelievable in its strength. Two decades of stored power from Grandma. Hattie Stern the buttoned-up, iron corset witch, letting go. Aunt Cass giving it everything she had. It felt like enough magic to move continents, to snatch the moon from the sky.

"I'm sorry, it's you my love," Hattie said.

"But you're the one," Aunt Cass said.

"It's all going to work out, Harlow," Grandma said.

Then the spell hit me and this time I wasn't knocked into a pitch black darkness, but rather swamped with light, brilliant and bright, like being cast into the sun itself.

AUTHOR NOTE

Read Wicked Witch (Torrent Witches #10) now!

Thanks for reading my book! More witch stories to come. If you'd like an email when a new book is released then you can sign up for my mailing list. I have a strict no spam policy and will only send an email when I have a new release.

I hope you enjoyed my work! If you have time, please write a review. They make all the difference to indie Authors.

In the next book the end is coming...

xx Tess

TessLake.com

Made in United States
Cleveland, OH
04 February 2026